PLAYLIST FOR A BROKEN HEART

Other books by Cathy Hopkins

Love At Second Sight

Series by Cathy Hopkins

Million Dollar Mates
Mates, Dates
Truth, Dare, Kiss or Promise
Cinnamon Girl
Zodiac Girls

PLAYLIST FOR A BROKEN HEART

CATHY HOPKINS

SIMON AND SCHUSTER

First published in Great Britain in 2014 by Simon and Schuster UK Ltd
A CBS COMPANY

1 3 5 7 9 10 8 6 4 2

Simon & Schuster UK Ltd
1ˢᵗ Floor, 222 Gray's Inn Road
London
WC1X 8HB

Simon & Schuster Australia, Sydney

Simon & Schuster India, New Delhi

A CIP catalogue record for this book is available from the British Library.

PB ISBN: 978-1-4711-1791-6
EBook ISBN: 978-1-4711-1792-3

Printed and bound by CPI Group (UK) Ltd, Croydon, CR0 4YY

www.simonandschuster.co.uk
www.simonandschuster.com.au

Chapter One

'Here we go,' whispered Allegra.

I held my breath and waited for Mr Collins, our drama teacher, to read out who had got parts in the end-of-year play. Everyone who'd auditioned was standing near the wooden stage in the school hall. It smelt of beeswax and lavender from the polish used by the cleaners who'd started the evening clear-up behind us. *Please, please let me get Juliet*, I prayed.

I'd been rehearsing for weeks with my friend, Allegra, reading all the other parts so I could get it just right. She's a good mate and knows that it means a lot to me. I've come so close to getting a lead role in school productions before but never quite made it – always the bridesmaid, never the bride sort of thing. I also have an ulterior motive for wanting the lead female role this time and that is that I'm pretty sure that Alex Taylor, love of my life, though he doesn't know it yet, will probably play Romeo.

Everyone thinks it's in the bag that he'll get it because, apart from being a good actor, he's classically good-looking with soft brown hair that curls at his shoulders. If he gets the part, whoever plays opposite him will get to spend a lot of time with him. Normally I am not boy mad like Allegra and so many other girls my age. I think there's more to life than drooling over some stupid boy, but Alex is different. He's clever and motivated and just thinking about the scenes where Romeo and Juliet have to kiss makes my toes curl. So *please, please let Alex Taylor get the part of Romeo.*

Mr Collins glanced over our group, all of us ready to put on a cheerful face if we didn't get a part.

'Romeo. Alex Taylor,' he read. Alex, who was standing in front of me to the right, punched the air and grinned. I felt a rush of excitement – so far so good. Allegra glanced over and gave me the thumbs-up.

'Juliet. Paige Lord.'

Ohmigod. I'd got it! I felt elated and relieved at the same time. All that hard work had been worth it.

'Yay,' exclaimed Allegra and gave me a hug. I felt myself blush as everyone turned to look, even more so when Alex glanced round to see who I was. I immediately looked at the floor and cursed that I didn't have the nerve to look him in the eye and hold his gaze, the way an article about how to flirt in last week's *Teen Vogue* had advised. Make the connection, it had said. Look him in the eye that moment too long and, when you feel a charge of electricity, hold it another few moments and then look away. *So I've blown that*, I thought.

Up until today, I don't think Alex has even noticed me despite me accidentally-on-purpose walking past him a million times in the corridor. It's the only place I see him because he's in Year Twelve and I'm in Year Ten and the sixth formers have their own common room. But all that is about to change. Now that we're playing the lead roles, he has no choice but to notice me. We'll be acting the parts of one of the most famous romantic couples in history. We'll be rehearsing together for months, up until the performance just before we break up for the summer. I call that a result with a capital R.

When Allegra and I left school later, I was on cloud nine. It had been an excellent day. Besides hearing that I'd got the part of Juliet, some pieces from my art project had been chosen to hang in the reception hall. I'd been working on a series of portraits from some photographs I'd taken on the London streets over the Christmas holidays. On top of that, I'd got an A star for an English essay, and the cherry on the cake was that, after Mr Collins' announcement about the parts, Jason Rice, who would be Tybalt in the play, had suggested that the whole cast get together over the Easter holidays for a party at his house. My future had never looked brighter and it felt like I was about to embark on an exciting new chapter in my life.

'I knew you'd get it,' said Allegra. 'With your long dark hair and brown eyes, you have an Italian look. And you're tall like Alex so you'll look good together. Plus – don't take this the wrong way – you have a sort of innocence about you that I think worked in your favour too.'

'I have a sort of innocence about me because I *am* innocent! Not that I want to be. I mean, it's pathetic really. Fifteen and never had a proper boyfriend, unlike you, Miss Experienced.'

'You just haven't met the right boy. Playing opposite Romeo will be a good place to start, and for someone who's shy like you, it will be the perfect opportunity to get some confidence,' said Allegra. She was much more savvy about relationships than I was. Slim but curvy, blonde and cool, she attracted boys while I stood by, feeling tongue-tied and awkward. It was weird. I was fine if I was acting because it wasn't really me, so I didn't clam up like I did when I had to speak to boys in normal life. Acting a part in a play was like wearing a mask that I could hide behind.

'It will, won't it? It's a great chance to get in with Alex. Life would be perfect if Mum and Dad would sort out whatever it is that's been bugging them,' I said as we waited in the car park for her mum to pick us up. There had been a weird atmosphere at home lately, which of course I'd told Allegra all about because I had to talk to someone about it.

'How's that going?' Allegra asked. 'Still no idea what it's about?'

'The only thing I can think of that makes sense is that they're getting divorced,' I replied. I'd known that something was wrong with my parents for a few months, though nothing had been said. Dad had been more absent than usual and then quiet when he was home, whereas Mum was acting cheerful but something about her manner didn't ring true.

'Sounds like it,' she agreed. 'Are they arguing a lot?'

'Not that I've heard. But they both go silent the minute I enter the room as if they have a secret, but not a nice one like a surprise party or holiday. Whatever. I'm not going to let them ruin my mood.'

'Good because this is your day,' said Allegra. 'It's probably nothing. You know what parents are like – there's always something stupid bugging them. They're going to be over the moon when you give them your news.'

'They will,' I replied. I couldn't wait to get home and tell them.

Chapter Two

Mum and Dad were in the hall at home waiting for me when I arrived back from school.

'Where've you been, Paige?' asked Dad.

'Drama. I told Mum I'd be late. I got the part!' I said. I was dying to share my news but as I waited for the congratulations and questions, I saw that what I'd said hadn't registered with either of them.

'Come and sit down, Paige,' said Dad. 'We need to talk to you about something.'

'Let her get a cup of tea or something,' said Mum. 'She's only just got in.'

They were both acting so seriously, it was beginning to freak me out.

'No. I'm fine,' I said. 'I don't need anything. Just

tell me what's happened. Has someone died? Gran or Grandpa?'

'Nothing like that,' said Mum. 'Let's all go into the sitting room.' I followed them in from the hall and we sat down, Mum and Dad next to each other on the sofa and me in one of the armchairs opposite. All of us took a deep breath and the room felt heavy with the weight of the unspoken words in the air.

A feeling of dread hit me as I looked at their faces. I had to break the uncomfortable silence. 'I know what you're going to say,' I blurted.

Mum looked taken aback. 'You do?' she asked.

I nodded. 'You're getting a divorce. But before you do, have you thought of trying counselling?' A few girls in our class had parents who had got divorced so it was often the topic of conversation in school lunch breaks, and I remembered that Phoebe Marshall's parents had been to Relate then stayed together – until her mum ran off with her skiing coach.

A glimmer of a smile crossed Dad's face. 'We're not getting divorced, Paige. No getting rid of me that easy.'

'Ohmigod. One of you has cancer,' I said. Another classmate, Mary Philip's mum had breast cancer last year, but they got it in time and she's OK now. Maybe there was hope.

'No, we don't have cancer either,' said Dad. He looked at Mum again and gave a small shrug. 'Do you want to tell her or shall I?'

'I will,' said Mum. 'So, Paige. It's not so bad. It's er . . . it's just that . . . our circumstances have changed. We . . .'

I listened as words came out of her mouth and then Dad's, but as they spoke I felt like part of me left the room. My body was there, ears listening, eyes seeing, but everything took on a dreamlike quality, not real at all. I got the gist of what they were telling me though. My whole life was going to change big time. *Big* time. And not in a good way.

I've never been totally clear on what Dad actually does, although he's tried to explain a number of times. Finances. Something to do with shares and investments. He's always done well at it, that I do know, because we live in a fabulous detached house with a huge garden by the river in Richmond. Dad drives a Mercedes, Mum a Porsche. I go to one of the best private schools in the country and we have two five-star holidays a year. Not any more, I was hearing. Dad's lost everything and had to declare himself bankrupt.

What? That's not possible, I thought, then told myself to keep listening. This was important. Some investments went badly wrong, and he'd put the house up as collateral, and it seems we've lost that too and we have to vacate in a month's time. Nothing is left but a big bad debt.

I felt totally in shock, like someone had just knocked a hole in me.

'We *can't* have lost everything,' I said. 'It can't be true.'

'I'm afraid it is,' said Dad.

'But you must have savings?'

'All gone,' said Dad.

'So . . . so what does this mean exactly?' I asked.

Dad glanced over at Mum. I'd never seen him like this before – uncertain, unshaven and pale. Usually he was Mr Sure of Himself, out the door at six in the morning, dressed in a suit and tie, dark hair slicked back and shining. He had a glow about him. A glow that said, 'I am a successful and very wealthy man'. Not today though. Today he looked dejected, broken even.

'It means we're going to be moving,' Mum said with a false smile, her voice in the higher pitch she always used when she wasn't happy about something. As I studied her, she looked her usual immaculate self, her make-up impeccable, her highlighted blonde hair freshly blow-dried as it was always was on a Friday, ready for the weekend. However, I could see shadows under her eyes like she hadn't slept properly. 'We're going to go to Bath to live with my sister.'

'Moving? To Bath? Aunt Karen?'

Mum nodded.

'For how long?'

'Until . . .' Mum looked at Dad. 'Until we can make other arrangements.'

'But that's insane,' I blurted.

'That it may be, but that's what's happening,' said Dad wearily.

'Do you mean for a few days or weeks?' I asked.

'A permanent move, Paige,' said Mum. 'We're leaving London.'

'Permanent? *No*. But why? This is our home. When? It doesn't make sense. This is a wind-up, isn't it? You're having me on.'

'I wish we were,' said Mum. 'We'll be going in a few weeks.'

'Few weeks? *No*. I can't leave my school now.'

Mum looked like she was going to cry and I felt as if I might too. 'It's the last thing we want to happen, believe me Paige, but luckily we've found a school in Bath that has the same syllabus. It's called Queensmead. It has a very good reputation.'

I didn't want to hear about a new school. I didn't want to hear about moving – especially not today, which had been the best day of my life until I got home. 'No. Dad, you can fix it can't you?'

'Not this time, baby girl,' said Dad sadly. 'Believe me, I've tried, I really have, and I'm afraid we have no choice. We have to go.'

'Can't Gran or Grandpa lend you money?'

Dad shook his head. 'Not the amount we need, and anyway I wouldn't take their savings, especially not at this time of their lives.'

This could not be happening. Not now. I was going to be Juliet. Alex was going to be Romeo. I liked my school. I liked our life. 'But why can't we move in London? Everyone we know is here. We *have* to stay. What about school?'

'We can't afford to stay in London and we can't afford the school fees any more,' said Mum in a clipped voice.

'But you've paid until the end of the year, haven't you? So I have to stay.'

'Due to the circumstances, the school has been kind enough to reimburse the fees for the last term,' said Dad.

I felt a wave of anxiety as I pictured the scene – Dad

12

having to go to my headmaster. It must have been excruciating for him.

'Bath will be great, Paige. You'll love it. It will be a new start for all of us. A new place, new people to meet, and it will be lovely spending some time with Karen and her family. It's been ages since we had some proper time with her. I bet we won't miss London for a second once we get settled in.' She couldn't fool me. She smiled but it didn't reach her eyes.

'Are you saying that we're . . . we're poor?'

Mum glanced nervously at Dad. 'Not poor exactly,' she said. 'Just our circumstances have changed and we have to make some cutbacks.'

Moving in with Aunt Karen. Losing our lovely house. That sounds like poor to me, I thought as I looked at Dad, willing him to take charge, but he was just staring at the floor as though he wished he could be anywhere else but here with Mum and I having this conversation.

My mind went into a spin as the implications hit me. Moving meant leaving my friends, Allegra, my bedroom with the window that looked out over the river. I'd be leaving my life. And *Alex Taylor*. Alex Taylor, and just after he'd noticed me. It was too cruel. Tragic.

And live with Aunt Karen? There were six of them, eight if you counted the dog and cat. Aunt Karen, Uncle Mike, Tasmin, Jake, Joe and Simon. We hadn't ever stayed over with them the few times we'd visited because they didn't have room, and we hadn't even been down that way for years, not since I was nine or ten. Not that Mum isn't close to her sister, she is – they're always on the phone to each other – but everyone gets together at Christmas or for birthday celebrations at Gran and Grandpa's in Surrey. How could we possibly be going to live with Aunt Karen and Uncle Mike? From what I remembered, they'd moved since we were there and their new house sounded tiny. Terraced. Four bedrooms and one bathroom. We had four bathrooms, one each for Mum, Dad and I and one for the guest suite.

'But there's no room there. There are six of them in that minuscule house,' I said.

'It will only be temporary, until your dad and I get jobs and we can find our own place to live,' said Mum.

'*You're* going to work?' I asked.

Mum has never worked, not in a job. Not that she was idle. She was always doing something – Pilates on a Monday, watercolour painting on Tuesday, cooking class on Wednesday, ladies' lunch on Thursday followed by a meeting for one of the charities she runs, and Friday shopping, the hairdresser's and beautician with her friend. She was always busy but she'd never had a paid job. She hadn't needed to.

Mum nodded. 'I'll find something.' As she said this, I saw Dad wince.

'*I'll* find something,' he said. 'I'll get us out of this mess.'

Mum leant over, took his hand and squeezed it. 'I know you will, Patrick.'

'I'm sorry, Paige,' Dad said to me, then put his head in his hands for a few moments. I wasn't sure which was more shocking, seeing my father behave like this or the fact that we'd be leaving London and the house where we'd lived all my life to live in some unfamiliar place in the middle of nowhere. I hadn't seen much of Bath when we had been there, only the area where Aunt Karen lived, and it looked really boring. London was the place to be, everyone knew that. London was *my* place to be.

It. Could. Not. Be. Happening.

'But you *must* have some money somewhere,' I said.

'Not any more,' said Mum.

'Can't you borrow some from a bank?'

'I wish it was that easy,' said Dad.

Mum took a deep breath and sat up straight. 'Come on. Let's remember who we are. We're the Lord family. We're survivors. We'll get through this. Life's a rollercoaster, up and down we go. We're going down for a while but things will turn around and we'll be going up again before you know it.'

Dad sat up straight too. 'Course we will,' he said. 'Things will turn around but, in the meantime, you'll have to be a brave girl, Paige. I need you to be strong and not be too upset about the changes coming. Change is part of life and you have to embrace it and go with it or it will destroy you.'

I got the feeling he was talking to himself as well as me. But it couldn't really be happening. Something would make things all right. We couldn't have lost everything. Things like this didn't happen to people like us.

Mum stood up. 'Would you like a hot drink now, Paige?' she asked.

As if that will make everything all right, I thought, but I nodded anyway. I felt stunned by their news.

Dad got up and left the room.

As I sat there, trying to take in the enormity of what they had just told me, I felt cold. So, not divorce. No. This was much, *much* worse.

Chapter Three

I awoke the next day in my queen-size bed. My room had been decorated last year – a soft lavender colour with mauve velvet curtains and bedspread. My dressing table and stool were over by the window, a bookshelf packed with my favourite books by my desk on the other side, and opposite my bed was a wall-to-wall wardrobe. It looked fab, everything in its place. The curtains weren't fully drawn, the sun was pouring in and, for a moment, everything seemed normal, safe and cosy. A lovely spring Saturday morning and I could have a lie-in. As I snuggled down under the covers, my mobile beeped that I had a message.

It was from Allegra. *You OK?*

The conversation with Mum and Dad yesterday evening came flooding back. For a brief second it had seemed like a bad dream but the reality soon hit me. I'd called Allegra the moment I'd got upstairs last night and, like me, she couldn't believe it. I'd also found it hard to admit the whole truth to her. I felt a whole mix of emotions: embarrassed at our situation, sad, sorry and ashamed. Like Mum had done last night, instead of stating the fact that we are now poor, I found myself using her more diplomatic words – our circumstances have changed, it's a temporary measure.

It felt weird. I'd always told Allegra everything and part of me wanted to wail down the phone. This. Can't. Be. Happening. But another part of me had gone into shock and couldn't let any real feeling out until I made more sense of it all in my head. Not that Allegra is snooty about money or anything, or at least I don't think she is, but then I'd never been in this situation before. I had a privileged life, as did everyone in my school. I quickly texted her back that I'd speak to her later, then I got up, put on my dressing gown and headed downstairs.

Mum was sitting at the table with a cup of coffee in the kitchen. She looked up as I walked in.

'How are you, love?' she asked, her concern for me showing on her face.

I slumped down opposite. 'It's a lot to take in. Being told that my . . . I mean *our* whole world has changed and yet here we are, sun shining into our top-of-the-range kitchen, us sitting at the table like nothing's happened. I can't get my head around it.'

She nodded. 'I know. It must be hard for you. Your dad and I have lived with it a bit longer and, although that doesn't make it easier, we've had some time to adjust. Both of us feel really bad about having to take you out of school on top of everything else.'

'Why do we have to go so soon?'

'It's not really soon. Things have been difficult for months but came to a head recently. Your father didn't want to say anything before, not until he'd explored every avenue to get us out of this mess, in case some miracle happened, but it didn't and it seems there is no way out. As you know your dad's already spoken to your headmaster—'

'About the fees?'

'And you leaving, so you . . . you don't have to go back at all if you don't want. You'd have been breaking up next week for the Easter holidays anyway.'

'Not go back at all? Why not? I'll want to say good-bye to everyone. Oh . . . but what will I tell them?' I remembered my conversation with Allegra.

Mum looked at me tenderly. 'It could be awkward for you,' she said.

'But I'll have to tell Mr Collins that I can't play Juliet after all. He'll have to give the part to someone else.' *Mia Jeffrey probably*, I thought and an image of her with Alex flashed through my mind. *So* not fair.

Mum sighed. 'Oh Paige, you got the part.'

'I told you last night.'

'Did you?' Mum's eyes filled with tears. 'I didn't take it in. Believe me, both your father and I had been dreading telling you what's happened. I do feel we've let you down so badly. I can't tell you how sorry I am, and if there was anything I could have done, you know I would.' She sniffed back tears, got up to go to the sink and looked out the window so I wouldn't see her face.

Seeing Mum upset made me realise that this wasn't just about me. 'Maybe we can come back here some time,' I said. 'When Dad's sorted it all out.'

'Unlikely,' she said without turning around. 'But never say never, hey?'

*

The following weeks were a blur of sorting, packing and trying to accept that we really were moving. Mum told me more about the school I'd be starting at in Bath after the Easter holidays, though I still didn't want to hear or believe it. I was amazed that Dad and her had sorted it so quickly but it seemed that, unbeknown to me, so many arrangements had been going on behind the scenes for a few months.

Allegra was round every day before we left, or I went over to her place. She had soon grasped what was really going on. We talked it over again and again and she was totally cool about the fact that we didn't have any money any more. 'Happens to loads of people,' she said. 'I bet your dad will get it together again.' I wasn't so sure. He went about the place like a robot and looked even more in shock than I was. Allegra asked her mum if I could go and live with them but my mum wouldn't hear of it. She looked so sad when I put the idea to her that I didn't pursue it. Allegra and I swore we'd be friends forever though, and would Skype and text daily as we had always done.

I did go into school again but only for a few days to get my things and talk to a few teachers about various projects I hadn't finished. They were all very kind, which made it worse and made me want to just leave.

I knew I had no option and there didn't seem to be any point in prolonging the agony, that part of my life was over. Also, I dreaded seeing Alex and knowing what could have been but now would never be. However, as luck would have it, I bumped into him on my last day when he was coming out of the canteen and Allegra and I were walking along the corridor.

'Hey, Paige,' he said when he saw me.

I blushed and felt flattered that he'd remembered my name. 'Oh. Hi, I mean hey,' I managed to get out.

'I hear you're leaving?'

I nodded and desperately wished I could think of something witty or interesting to say, but looking into his eyes made my mind go blank. He had such beautiful grey-green eyes.

'So we won't be playing opposite each other after all?'

I shook my head. 'Nuh.'

He shrugged. 'Bad timing, hey?'

I nodded. Words seemed to have totally escaped me.

Allegra came to my rescue as always. 'She's going to live in Bath,' she said.

Alex didn't take his eyes off me. 'Bath?'

Allegra moved away a distance. 'I'll catch you later,' she said. 'I've er . . . got a thing.'

Over Alex's shoulder, she turned, grinned and gave me the thumbs-up. Alex continued to look into my eyes.

'Yes. Bath. Somerset,' I managed to get out. 'We go after Easter.'

'I know Bath. I know it well. Used to live there before we came here and I often go back to see my cousin and mates. You'll like it. Wow. So soon . . . Well, good luck, Paige.'

'Uh. Thanks.' He's kind to say that I'd like Bath, I thought, though I knew I wouldn't.

Alex looked reluctant to go and, as he continued to look into my eyes, I felt an ache of longing. He really did have lovely eyes. He smiled down at me. 'Parting is such sweet sorrow,' he said, quoting Juliet from the play, then looked at me as if he wanted me to finish the line. I knew it so well but the words wouldn't come.

'That I shall say goodnight till it be morrow.' He finished the line for me. We both smiled and it felt as if we were in a bubble, all alone and away from the rest of the world, school and its many pupils rushing by us in the corridor. He continued with another quote from the play, this time one of Romeo's. 'Farewell, farewell! One kiss, and I'll descend.'

I suddenly remembered my lines and felt a surge of energy.

'Art thou gone so? Love, lord, ay, husband, friend!
I must hear from thee every day in the hour,
For in a minute there are many days:
O, by this count I shall be much in years
Ere I again behold my Romeo!'

I put every bit of what I was feeling into the lines and could see he felt it too.

'Farewell. I will omit no opportunity
That may convey my greetings, love, to thee,'

said Alex, continuing as Romeo. His lines were full of the passion that was fitting for the star-crossed lovers and his eyes twinkled as if he was enjoying our exchange.

'O think'st thou we shall ever meet again?'

I asked. Alex put his hand on my arm.

'I doubt it not; and all these woes shall serve
For sweet discourses in our time to come.'
'O God, I have an ill-divining soul!'

I said with a sigh. I was really getting into the part now, finding it so easy to talk to him with someone else's words.

> 'Methinks I see thee, now thou art below,
> As one dead in the bottom of a tomb:
> Either my eyesight fails, or thou look'st pale.'

'And trust me, love, in my eye so do you,' Alex quoted. 'Dry sorrow drinks our blood. Adieu, adieu!'

He reached up and touched my chin, a gesture so gentle and yet it made my heart thud in my chest. Suddenly he grinned. 'Shame, Paige,' he said. 'We'd have been good together.'

I nodded and blushed. *We'd* have been good together? Did he mean as a couple? Alex and Paige, or acting Romeo and Juliet? *I guess I'll never know now*, I thought as he looked away.

'Take care of yourself,' he said, then turned, and a second later he was gone.

I stood there in shock and it wasn't long before Allegra came back to join me.

'I . . . I just had a moment with Alex. A *moment* moment. There was chemistry.'

'I know,' said Allegra and she grinned. 'I saw.'

*

On our last day, I felt as if I was floating. Despite the fact that all around me familiar items had disappeared into boxes and cases, a part of me kept thinking something would happen to make it right, a fairy godmother come to the rescue. If Alex could speak to me and look into my eyes, miracles did happen; but no, the removal men arrived and the last of my safe and secure world was carried out the door by eight men in yellow overalls. Carpets, rugs, sofas and furniture were going in the vans then into a storage warehouse somewhere down the motorway. Mum, Dad and I would be travelling by car and had suitcases with the bare minimum of belongings.

Allegra came to say a final goodbye. 'I'll come back to see you soon,' I said as we stood on the porch at the front of our house.

'And I'll come down to Bath as soon as I can,' she said. 'I promise.'

I tried to make myself smile but couldn't hold back the tears. 'Laters.'

'Laters,' said Allegra. She had tears in her eyes too.

We hugged goodbye then it was time for her to go. As I watched her walk away, it felt as if my stomach was full of knives, all cutting into me. Allegra had been my best friend since my first day in Year Seven.

Apart from holidays abroad with our families, I'd seen her every day for almost four years. She was part of me and I couldn't imagine life without her.

When the removal men had closed up the back of their vans and gone, Mum and I went round the empty rooms checking that there was nothing left. It felt eerie and empty and, without the furnishings that had always been there to soften sound, the rooms echoed our footsteps. I was trying my best to be cheerful because, as time had gone on, it had really hit home how hard the move was for Mum and Dad as well as me, and me blubbing wouldn't help. Mum was still doing her cheerful act but, when we'd done the rounds of the house and she'd shut the front door and locked it, she looked like she was going to cry. Dad went to get the car and Mum and I stood a moment in the front garden. She looked up at the bare windows on the first floor and then her tears did come.

'I can't believe I'll never go in there again, my home,' she said. 'Or see my garden, my lovely roses bloom this year.'

I put my arms around her and she hugged me tight.

'It's only until we find a place of our own again,' I said. 'We'll be back on our feet in no time.'

The look she gave me broke my heart. A smile that said, 'You just don't get it, do you?' But I did.

Dad brought round the car to the front and Mum and I climbed in. It was a Volkswagen Polo. The Porsche and Mercedes had gone weeks ago. I'd noticed that the cars weren't in their usual spots on the drive but had assumed they were in for service, never imagining for a minute that they'd gone for good, but that was before I knew the truth.

Dad didn't glance back at the house but Mum and I both looked out the back window as we drove away as if trying to hang on to our life there. I felt broken-hearted. The car turned the corner and the house was gone.

Mum gazed out of the window at the traffic. 'And so life flows on,' she said as we drove through Richmond towards Kew and out to the M4 where Dad hit the fast lane towards Bath.

A new chapter for all of us, I thought as I tried to push images of Alex Taylor's face out of my mind. *I wonder what it will hold?*

Chapter Four

Mystery Boy

'Who ever loved that loved not at first sight?'
Shakespeare: *As You Like It* – Act 3, Scene 5.

A girl. A girl in the park. She's walking her dog –
though by the way the dog is pulling on the lead, the
dog is walking her. She has chestnut-coloured hair,
glossy in today's sun. She's wearing jeans and a red
jacket. She never notices me, though I've seen her
around a few times. There's something about her.
The way she moves. A lightness. A grace. A bright-
ness about her face. Sometimes she's on her phone,
sometimes she's talking to her dog. I wish she'd talk
to me. She looks like fun to be with, as if she'd have
a lot to say. Seeing her makes me feel alone although

I'm not. I know tons of people. I'd like to approach her but I don't know how, though normally I can talk for England. She makes me feel awkward and dumb. I can't do it. I feel like I'd babble and blush and look a fool.

My far-away girlfriend. Is she out of my league?

Chapter Five

My brave face lasted about five minutes once we'd got to Aunt Karen's. Not that Aunt Karen wasn't friendly – she was and she greeted each of us with a big hug then ushered us inside. She's four years younger than Mum and they're like chalk and cheese in looks. Mum is impeccable and slim in her classic designer clothes, usually navy and cream, Aunt Karen is curvier in well-worn jeans, colourful tops and trainers, and her shoulder-length auburn hair is as unruly as Mum's blonde bob is tamed. Uncle Mike was dressed in a similar casual style in jeans and a red fleece.

My four cousins, Tasmin, Jake, Joe and Simon, were squashed on a sofa watching TV. Uncle Mike had tea and biscuits ready for us. I smiled at Tasmin and she gave me a brief nod by way of reply – a greeting of sorts, but not very friendly considering I've known her most of my life and we'd always got on. I hadn't seen her since a family wedding a few years ago. She was fresh-faced and chatty and we'd had fun hanging out with the other teens. Since then, she's got curvier, sulky-looking and, although the same age as me, she looked about twenty.

The TV programme *Snog, Marry or Avoid* came into my head as I took in her fake tan, false eyelashes, heavily made-up eyes and the dyed long blonde hair that looked like extensions. The programme shows a before and after beauty treatment where the presenters do a reverse makeover and get girls who overdo the slap to look more like themselves and less like drag artists. *Tasmin would really benefit from a more natural look*, I thought as Tasmin looked at me with equal dismay. She was dressed in tights, denim shorts, trainers and a tight red top. I guess I looked super-straight to her in my white shirt and jeans, hair tied back and no make-up apart from a touch of mascara and lip gloss. Mum had drummed it into me that less is more when it comes to make-up.

'Switch that television off,' said Aunt Karen to

Jake, the eldest. Reluctantly he did as he was told then slumped back on the sofa. They'd obviously all been told to be there to greet us. Uncle Mike poured tea and Dad looked as miserable as I felt as we sat together on the other sofa in the room making weak attempts at conversation, though Mum looked happy to see her sister. I noticed that Uncle Mike had odd socks on, one blue, one grey. The room looked lived in, with games, DVDs, books, magazines and school-books on every surface.

After fifteen minutes of catching up on each other's latest news, Uncle Mike insisted on taking Dad down to the pub.

'You look like you need a stiff drink, mate,' he said to him and whisked Dad away, leaving Mum and I to my cousins, more tea and biscuits. The boys were sweet enough – Jake with his mother's wavy hair was twelve and clearly going to be a heartbreaker; Joe, who was ten, was more shy than the others; and Simon, the youngest at seven, was full of energy and enthusiasm for our stay.

'And are you going to stay here forever?' he asked. 'Mum said you're homeless. Have you been sleeping on the streets in London? I have a tent you can borrow if you like.'

'Shhh, Simon,' said Aunt Karen. 'They're not homeless. They have us.'

Mum looked at the floor during this exchange while I tried to gauge how my cousin, Tasmin was feeling. It was hard to tell because her face showed nothing but boredom. As Mum and Aunt Karen caught up with family gossip, the boys began to look restless and soon drifted away upstairs. Tasmin kept looking at her mother, who ignored her. I got the feeling that she'd been told to stay and be sociable, although she wasn't making any effort to talk to me and I wasn't in the mood for being chatty either. I felt shell-shocked at the speed with which my life had changed. In the last few weeks in London, even though the house was being packed up, it felt unreal. Now we'd done the drive and were sitting in Aunt Karen's house, our suitcases in the hall, there was no more denying the reality and I felt overwhelmingly sad about the loss of life as I'd known it.

Finally Aunt Karen took notice of the awkward silence. 'Tasmin, can you show Paige where she's going to be sleeping,' she instructed.

'Umpf,' said Tasmin. Or some word like that. She got up and with a jerk of her chin indicated that I should follow her upstairs.

'Shall I bring my bag?' I asked.

'Well I'm not carrying it up for you,' said Tasmin. 'I'm not a servant.'

'Tasmin,' said Aunt Karen. 'Don't be rude.'

Tasmin looked pleadingly at her mum then back at me. 'Well there's nowhere for you to put stuff but you can bring it up, I guess.'

'Tasmin, I told you to clear some space in the wardrobe and a couple of drawers,' said Aunt Karen.

'I tried, but where I am I supposed to put *my* things?' asked Tasmin. 'We're short of space as it is in this house.'

Aunt Karen glared at her but she shrugged and went up the stairs that led off the sitting room. I got my case from the narrow hallway then followed her up. I got the message loud and clear. She was no happier with the new arrangements than I was.

On the first-floor landing, she pushed open a bedroom door. It had a sign on it in black letters. KEEP OUT ON PAIN OF DEATH. PRIVATE. Underneath was a skull-and-bones image. I went in after her. It was a small boxroom, painted pink, with a chest of drawers, wardrobe and full-length mirror which was surrounded by pages showing fashion shoots that had been cut out from magazines and Blu-Tacked to the wall. It smelt sweet and girlie – of strawberries and hairspray. There were clothes everywhere, on hangers behind the door, piled over the end of Tasmin's bed, strewn on a chair behind the door. I saw that a campbed had been made up for me on the right of the room opposite hers on the left.

'Home sweet home,' said Tasmin. 'Your five-star luxury accommodation.'

'Look. I'm really sorry about this,' I said. 'It's only for a while. We'll be gone as soon as Dad sorts something.'

Tasmin raised an eyebrow. 'Yeah right,' she said. 'We'll see. But as long as you're here, there are some ground rules.' She pointed to her bed then mine. 'My side, your side. There's room on a couple of hangers in the wardrobe but I suggest you keep most of your stuff in your case. And I don't want you borrowing anything of mine, OK?'

As if, I thought and nodded, then slung my bag on my bed.

Tasmin didn't hang around. She changed her trainers and five minutes later I heard the front door slam. I looked out the window to see her tottering out the gate and along the road. She didn't look comfortable in the strappy high-heels she'd put on. I thought about calling Allegra, but to say what? 'I've landed in Loserville, get me out of here.' I didn't want her feeling sorry for me. I decided to wait until things were more settled, if ever.

While the others were downstairs, I decided to have a look around the top floors. Although we'd visited Aunt Karen a few times when I was younger, they moved to this house only last year so I wasn't familiar with the layout.

There were four bedrooms. Aunt Karen's and Uncle Mike's had a double bed but, like Tasmin's, there was stuff on every surface and a keyboard, guitar and amp in the corner of the room. The instruments must belong to Uncle Mike. He worked as a music teacher and used to be in a band when he was younger.

The third tiny bedroom, which had clearly been used as a study, was the tidiest of the rooms so far and had a futon on the floor, which I presumed was for Mum and Dad. There was no room on either side for even a chest of drawers, so God knows where they were going to put their stuff. I felt tears sting my eyes at the thought of them squashed in there on the fold-out bed. How different to their beautiful room back home with its marble en-suite bathroom that was three times the size of this tiny make-do room. But the house in Richmond wasn't 'back home' any more, was it?

I sniffed back my tears. *I am not going to get upset over this*, I told myself as I looked in the bathroom. It was simple enough; white with a wooden floor, a bath with shower and curtain in it. The loo was in a separate room next door. Thank heavens for that, I thought. It would have been awful if the loo had been in the bathroom, with the number of people living here. Up another narrow flight of stairs was the fourth and largest bedroom with bunk beds at one end and a single bed under the eaves at the other. Like the sitting room, there was stuff everywhere: books, toys, games and clothes all over the place. It smelt of unwashed socks. *Must be the boys' room*, I thought as I closed the door.

Going back down the stairs, I felt angry about our situation and sad at the same time. I didn't know what to do with the feelings and they seemed to have locked inside of me, leaving me numb. I couldn't be angry with Mum or Dad. I could see how hard this move had hit them and we'd always been told at school that to be miserable because things weren't going your way was a waste of time. If times were tough, you could sink or swim. It was true. I could be miserable as hell but it wasn't going to change things. I had no option but to swim, to make the best of it, and that's exactly what I was going to do, Tasmin or no Tasmin, rotten luck or not.

I went back onto the ground floor and saw Aunt Karen was looking at Mum with concern and holding her hand. On the coffee table in front of them was a bottle of wine and two glasses. I could tell from the way they were sitting close on the sofa that they were having a heart-to-heart. *Not a time to interrupt*, I thought and tiptoed into the kitchen. It wasn't as bad as I'd expected and was a large light space, with a dining table to the right, next to glass doors that opened out to a terrace and small fenced-off garden. I could see Simon and Joe kicking about a football with a small dog trying to join in and barking at their heels. A cat came out from under the table and meowed pleadingly. I looked around for cat food, found a box of dry food and put some out. *God, there's nowhere to get away from anyone here*, I thought as I wondered what to do with myself next. I'd had enough tea to last a lifetime so I decided to creep back upstairs and unpack what I could.

When I got back up there, I went over to look out of the window. I'd fallen asleep for the last half-hour of the journey down so hadn't really noticed where we were or seen anything of Bath as we drove through. The weather had changed since we'd arrived and it was grey and dismal. I noticed a sudden movement below to my right. Someone was on the path leading out of the house next door. I drew back so that I couldn't be seen. A tall slim boy with tousled brown hair who looked about seventeen or eighteen was walking a blonde girl out to the road.

At the gate, they stopped, then after saying something, she wrapped her arms around him and they kissed goodbye. She seemed reluctant to leave and, after a while, he pulled back, looked at his watch then playfully pushed her away. She pouted as if she didn't want to leave, so he kissed her again, briefly this time, then said something. I couldn't hear, but from his body language, it looked like he was telling her he had things to do, had to go. She finally went on her way and the boy disappeared back into his house. I watched the girl walk off down the street and soon she disappeared too. I was about to turn back when I noticed that the boy had reappeared.

He crept along the path back to the street and checked that the girl had gone. Then he waved at someone coming towards him. *Hmm, he's cute-looking, I thought as I watched.* At first I thought the girl was returning but, when I looked closer, I saw that it was a different girl. This one had long titian-coloured hair. Her face lit up when she got closer to the boy, who was also grinning at her. They put their arms around each other and went for a passionate snog.

When they pulled back, he took her by the hand to go inside his house. I noticed that he checked the road again and, I couldn't help it, I leant forward to see if girl number one might be returning. My movement must have caught the boy's eye because he suddenly glanced up at the window. I quickly drew back and hoped he hadn't seen me. When I peeked back, seconds later, there was no sign of him or the girl. *Hmm, interesting*, I thought. *He might be cute but he's clearly a love rat and two-timing those girls.*

I went back to looking at the landscape in front of me. In London, we had a stunning view of trees and the river Thames winding its way towards London. Here, the land was flat, a row of semi-detached houses opposite. I vaguely remembered from visits when I was little that Bath had hills around it. *Maybe that was somewhere else*, I told myself. My main memory of here when I was small was of playing in a park with swings and slides, but it was so long ago I can't remember too much about that either apart from the fact that Tasmin was sweet back then.

An ambulance raced by, sirens blaring. Mum had said something about Aunt Karen's house being near the hospital so that must be where it was headed. I turned away from the window, went and lay on my bed and looked around Tasmin's room. *How have I landed here?* I asked myself as I took in the scarves hanging on the wardrobe handle, the make-up, nail polish and hair straighteners cluttering the space in front of the mirror on the chest of drawers. *This is so clearly someone else's room, someone I don't know that well any more. I don't belong here. No wonder Tasmin stomped out.*

I got up, unpacked a few things and looked for somewhere to put them. There didn't seem to be any room anywhere so I put them back in my case and shoved it at the bottom of the bed.

A moment later, Mum came up and sat opposite me on Tasmin's bed. 'You OK?'

'She hates me,' I said.

'No she doesn't. She's a headstrong girl, always was, and if you see it from her point of view, she's just lost her privacy.'

I indicated the room with my hands. 'Duh.'

'I know, you have too.' She looked around the room and sighed. 'We won't be here long, I promise you that. I mean, it's a perfectly nice house and everything . . .'

'But not what we're used to,' I finished for her. 'Let's run away and get a room in a five-star hotel. There must be loads in Bath.'

'There are a few,' Mum replied, then she smiled wickedly. 'It's very tempting isn't it? And to think, only a few months ago, we'd have booked in without batting an eyelid.'

'I feel like we've landed in a parallel universe,' I said.

'I know. We have, my love, we have,' said Mum.

Dad and Uncle Mike had arrived back at eight with flushed red cheeks and reeking of beer. They were both snoring on the sofa half an hour later, much to the amusement of Jake, Joe and Simon. Jake tried to put a piece of rolled-up paper up his dad's nose until

Aunt Karen saw what he was doing and told him to leave him alone.

Tasmin didn't come home at all.

'Having a sleepover with a friend,' Aunt Karen explained as she made us all hot chocolates later that night before bed.

Can't say I blame her, I thought as I manoeuvred into a corner of the sofa next to Simon and Jake. I might have done the same if some alien had landed in the corner of my bedroom.

Later, I checked my Facebook page and there were loads of messages from friends back in London, wishing me luck and telling me to stay in touch. Already it seemed a million miles away. I did a search to find Alex Taylor's page. I just wanted to see his photo and remember the way he'd looked at me the last time I saw him. We weren't Facebook friends, and my finger hovered over the Add Friend link but I didn't. He'd probably forgotten all about me and, anyway, now some other Juliet was getting to look into his eyes and snog him in rehearsals.

I checked my mobile next. There were seven messages from Allegra getting increasingly insistent that I call her. She seemed a million miles away too and the thought of not seeing her every day made me feel desolate. I switched the phone off without replying. I was grateful that Tasmin wasn't coming back so I had at least one night alone in the perfumed, pink bedroom. There would be no one to hear me sob into my pillow.

Chapter Six

I woke to find the cat curled up on my bed. On seeing me wake, it got up, stretched, then came to nuzzle my nose. I noticed it was wearing a collar with an identity medal. Snowy, it said, which struck me as funny because the cat was black. It was comforting to have it purring softly in my ear.

I hadn't slept well. The pillows were lumpy and the duvet too heavy for the spring weather. Back home, Mum had always bought Egyptian cotton for our beds, with pillows and duvets made from Hungarian goose feathers, which were as light as clouds. They'd gone in storage with the rest of our things, but maybe Mum could retrieve the bed linen at least. *But that would probably make us look ungrateful or snobbish, I* thought as I lay there and stroked Snowy. Maybe not such a good idea.

There was a knock on the door. 'You decent?' called Aunt Karen.

'Yes,' I called back and the door opened and she came in. 'Is the cat a boy or girl?'

'Girl. She's a bit friendlier than Tasmin, hey? I am sorry about her behaviour – Tasmin's, that is, not the cat's!' she said. 'She's a good girl at heart and she'll come round. She's just a bit put out at having her space invaded.' She looked around the room. 'Usually no one's allowed in here. It's her very private hiding place from the rest of us.'

'Will she be back today?'

'She better had be. It's school tomorrow. Talking of which, I'm going to show your mum more of the local area so she can get her bearings – your school, the local shops and so on. Want to come?'

I shook my head. I felt a need to spend the morning on my laptop and Facebook seeing what my friends back home were up to, and I had to reply to Allegra. I couldn't avoid her forever. She'd sent another text this morning. *Task of the day*, it read. *Find 4 fit boys. Report back. Send photos on iPhone.* Typical Allegra. She probably thought that would cheer me up, but even if I did find any attractive boys, it would only remind me that my chance with Alex had gone with the rest of my old life, and if I did meet any new ones, I'd be back to being my usual tongue-tied self without Allegra there to break the ice. 'Maybe later?' I said to Aunt Karen.

'OK. Help yourself to breakfast when you're up,' she said. 'There's cereal and toast. Juice is in the fridge. And text us when you want to join us later.' She was about to leave, then turned back. 'I want you to make yourself at home, Paige, so please do. In the meantime, your mum needs a bit of a distraction so I might taking her shopping in town this after-noon too.'

'OK, that will be good,' I lied. Not that Mum didn't like shopping. She did. A lot. However, going round the shops might just rub it in that another aspect of our new life was that she could look but no longer buy what she wanted. 'Is Dad up?'

Aunt Karen nodded. 'Ages ago. Mike's taken him out in the car to help him get to know the area better and I think they're going to check out a few letting agencies too – see what's available, how much and so on. When you're ready to join your mum and me, turn left out of the house and keep going to the main road, then cross over, turn right and there's a row of shops. They're the nearest. We'll be somewhere along there – text me and I'll be more specific.'

The kitchen was a total mess when I got downstairs. *They obviously don't believe in keeping things tidy,* I thought as I began to move dirty dishes to the counter above the dishwasher. There were plates with half-eaten pieces of toast, jam jars with their lids off, cereal boxes, a milk spill. By the dining table was a shelving unit with just about every cereal on the market: porridge, muesli, Weetabix, Shredded Wheat, Cheerios, Kellogg's Crunchy mix, Coco Pops. *Something for everyone,* I thought as I began to stack the dishwasher.

After that, I put stuff away in cupboards then wiped the surfaces down. Having something to do and establishing some order made me feel slightly better. *Maybe symbolic,* I thought. *My whole life seems out of control but tidying up this small chaotic corner makes me feel like I do have some say after all.* I opened the back door and threw the uneaten toast out for the birds. The sun was shining and it felt good to feel its warmth on my face. To my right, I spotted Snowy who, on seeing me, rolled on her back and wriggled on the stone slabs of the patio. She was clearly enjoying the good weather too. As I stood in the garden, I noticed the boy from next door come out. I quickly darted back inside but I think he saw me before I could move out of sight.

After breakfast of toast and apricot jam, I went to look for one of the boys to give me the Wi-Fi password, but the house was deserted apart from Snowy who had come in and taken up her place on the sofa in the sitting room. I texted Allegra that I'd call her later, then decided to go and find Mum and Aunt Karen and check out my route to school. *Might as well, as there's nothing else to do*, I thought as I got ready, then followed the directions Aunt Karen had given me.

The sun was still shining when I set off along the suburban street where the semi-detached houses looked the same. All had small gardens at the front, most with off-street parking for two cars. *Positive, positive, must be positive*, I told myself. At the end of the road, I turned left, crossed over, turned right and soon found the row of shops Aunt Karen had told me about. Just ordinary shops, an estate agent (which I had a look in), a charity shop (which I didn't – we might be poor but we're not that desperate), a baker, a deli, then a café where I spotted Mum and Aunt Karen at the counter.

I opened the door and went in to join them. A group of boys at a table by the window checked me out – musicians by the look of the guitars by their table, maybe a couple of years older than me, and two of them were quite attractive in an indie kind of way. Allegra would have been pleased but it was hardly the place to get out my phone, point it at them and say. Smile for the photo, boys'. Aunt Karen was paying the bill so Mum and I went back out to the street.

'It doesn't look so bad here,' she said. She gestured at the street as we walked back up to the estate agent, where we both had a look at the houses for sale. 'Pick any house.'

I spotted a lovely old detached manor house in its own grounds that had a look of our home back in Richmond. Two point five million. 'That one,' I said.

Mum laughed and pulled me away. 'Moving on. You are your mother's daughter. Expensive taste. I think we might have to lower our standards for a while.'

'I'll try,' I said. 'But seriously, how long are we going to be staying with Aunt Karen?'

'Hard to say, Paige.'

'We will buy another house, won't we?'

Mum shook her head. 'Buying a house means getting a mortgage and the banks won't even consider your father now he's been declared bankrupt. They ask to see bank statements too and they don't look good at the moment. Renting might be an option if we can both get work. Then we'll just have to save – but I can tell you one thing, if and when we are ever ready to buy a house of our own again, it won't be in the million-pound range.'

'Aunt Karen said Dad was going to check out letting agencies.'

'He is but they might want to see proof of income and bank statements as well.'

'So we're stuck where we are,' I said

'Not for long if I can help it,' said Mum as Aunt Karen came to join us.

'Oh, you have to have a look in here,' she said and pulled Mum towards the charity shop. 'You can get some great bargains.'

Mum pulled a face at me over Aunt Karen's shoulder but she didn't pull away. I doubted she'd ever bought anything in a charity shop in her life. Nor had I and I certainly hadn't thought that lowering our standards, as Mum had just said, would mean having to buy other people's cast-offs.

'Maybe we can find something for you, Paige,' said Aunt Karen. 'They have brilliant stuff in here. Some of it new. The rich Bath ladies bring things here that they've never worn.'

Mum took a deep breath. I really felt for her. Not so long ago, she'd been one of those ladies. 'I'm game,' she said. 'Come on, Paige. Let's see what we can find.'

'I don't need anything,' I said. 'Really. I'll wait out here.'

'If you find anything you like, I'll treat you,' said Aunt Karen.

Mum gave me a look that said, 'Don't be ungrateful,' though she didn't need to. I knew it would be churlish to refuse and that I'd come across as stuck-up. The last thing I wanted to do was to upset Aunt Karen, or Mum for that matter, but to be given a mouldy item worn by an unknown stranger, then cast off, was so not what I considered a treat.

Inwardly I groaned as I noticed the boys from the café walking up the street towards us. I didn't want them to see me going into a charity shop like some sad loser but Mum gestured for me to join her so I pulled my hair over my face, put my head down and followed them in.

Once inside, we were greeted by a musty smell and rows and rows of shabby-looking clothes, racks of worn shoes, a display of mismatched crockery and glasses. Two old ladies were behind the counter having a cup of tea and a gossip about a mutual friend who'd just got out of hospital. Mum made a beeline for a shelf of books at the back whilst Aunt Karen browsed the clothes racks. I joined Mum and looked at the books and CDs. If I could find something to read, that would keep her and Aunt Karen happy. I certainly didn't want to buy anyone's old clothes.

I looked through the books for a while, then something on the floor tucked under the bottom shelf caught my eye – an open shoebox full of CDs. I mainly used my iPod these days but I had a flick through anyway. Most were artists I'd never heard of. Melanie. Neil Diamond. The Eagles. Halfway through, I came across one that said *Songs for Sarah* on the spine. I liked the title so I pulled it out. It was clearly a home-made compilation that had a DIY cover design with a montage of colourful images on the front – a girl's face and body broken up.

Just how I feel, I thought as I turned the case over. On the back was a black-and-white photograph. A boy in silhouette was looking out of a window. You couldn't see his face because he was in shadow. On the inside of the CD was a list of tracks. I glanced down it to see if I recognised any of the bands: Magus, Overheated, Citrus World, Random Strangers, Sainted, Black Pearl . . . No, none of them sounded familiar. I read the song titles next and, like the front cover, they seemed to echo how I was feeling. 'Stone in My Heart', 'The River Flows On', 'Forever Yours', 'Dreams of Yesterday', 'Masks of Tears and Smiles', 'Far-Away Friend', 'Dark and Distant' . . .

'Found something you want?' asked Aunt Karen coming up behind me.

I was about to put the CD back in the shoebox but then thought I might not find anything else I wanted and would actually like to hear how the tracks sounded.

'Er yes,' I said. 'This looks interesting but I haven't got a CD player.'

'It's yours,' she said with a grin. 'We have a few old CD players around the place – in fact there's one up in Tasmin's room. You could listen on that.'

I handed her the CD and she checked the price. 'Fifty pence. A bargain.'

She took it to the till, paid, then handed it back to me.

'There,' she said. 'A welcome to Bath CD.'

She looked so pleased to have got me something that I felt mean thinking the shop was for losers.

Outside the shop, the group of boys who had been in the café, were looking in the window. They came in a moment later and went to the window to look at a suitcase. It seemed in good condition. And so did the boys. One of them with blond surfer hair turned round, looked at me and winked. He was cute with big blue eyes and an open friendly face. Maybe charity shops weren't for losers after all.

Chapter Seven

Mystery Boy

'If music be the food of love, play on.'
Shakespeare: *Twelfth Night* – Act 1, Scene 1.

Exactly, Will, my old pal. Music. I shall make a CD for my girl in the park, a compilation, and give it to her. A CD is timeless. Something she can keep forever. I'll choose music that will speak to her heart. Music that will let her know that she is special. That I've seen that she stands out from the crowd. I can't find the words to speak to her. To approach her and just blab out some chat-up line would be boring anyway. She deserves better. The songs on the CD will say what my heart feels.

Chapter Eight

'Sorry I was such a prat yesterday,' said Tasmin when I opened the bedroom door later that afternoon.

After I'd been to the shops, I'd dumped my stuff then gone out again to have a further look around the area, but I hadn't got far because it had started pouring with rain.

Tasmin was sprawled on her bed listening to music with a friend, who was lying on mine like she owned it. I hoped she wasn't going to be as difficult as Tasmin had been. She was a stunning-looking black girl, tall with a mane of wild curly hair down past her shoulders, and everything about her said style. She had a red scarf with a bow at the front tied around her head and was wearing a yellow dress that nipped in at the waist with a wide red belt. The vintage look really suited her and in my usual jeans and white shirt I felt dull and boring compared to her

'Prat is Tasmin's middle name,' she said. She got up from my bed. 'Sorry, this is yours isn't it? Hi. I'm Clover. Welcome to Bath, though we call it Soggy Bottom. It rains a lot here.'

I liked her immediately.

She glanced over at my bed. 'Bummer of a story,' she said. 'Tas filled me in a bit, said you were mega loaded before.'

I shrugged. 'I guess.'

'And I am sorry Tas was a Class A bitch when you arrived – she filled me in on that too so I apologise for her.'

Tasmin got up and switched off the CD player. 'Excuse me, I am in the room,' she said. 'I can apologise for myself and, in fact, just did if you'd been listening, and . . . well you can see there's not much room here and you coming is like my whole world's been turned upside down.'

'Tell me about it,' I agreed.

Tasmin took the CD out of the player, put it back in its case and handed it to me. 'Er . . . this is yours. I saw it at the end of your bed. I hope you don't mind.'

It was the CD from the charity shop. 'No. It . . .' I bit the words back. I'd been about to say it wasn't even a CD I wanted, I'd only got it to please Aunt Karen, but then realised how rude that would have sounded. 'No, no, course it's fine. I haven't listened to it yet.'

'There are some nice tracks on it,' said Clover. 'You should give it a listen.'

Tasmin was staring at me and it was beginning to make me feel uncomfortable. 'It must have been tough for you,' she finally said. 'I'm . . . not usually so insensitive . . . like I was yesterday.' Clover rolled her eyes when she said this and Tasmin laughed. 'OK, er . . . maybe I am. Clover says it's because I'm an Aries – speak before I think, leap before I look and all that. Clover's Libran, ever the diplomat. I remember your house in London. It was amazing.'

'It was.'

'Like what?' asked Clover.

'A mansion, huge rooms, loads of bathrooms,' said Tasmin.

'It was . . . by the river. It was nice,' I added.

'Nice?' said Tasmin. 'Paige, you're so reserved. Your house was awesome. When I was little, I used to dream of running away to come and live with you.'

'Did you?' I asked. This was news to me.

'So what the hell happened?' asked Tasmin as Clover joined her on her bed.

I shrugged. 'Not sure. Bad investment or . . . not bad, Dad wouldn't do that. Something unexpected happened on the stock market. Some shares plummeted, and not just Dad's. He advised people as well and they lost money too. I can't say I really understand it all.'

'Yeah, Mum said it was something to do with stocks and shares,' said Tasmin. 'Apparently it's like gambling. Sometimes you win, sometimes you lose. Your dad lost. So, I guess we're stuck with each other for the time being and have to make the best of it, right?'

'I'd like that,' I said.

Tasmin cracked up. 'You are *so* posh and polite.'

'Yeah,' said Clover, 'you could learn from her.'

Tasmin biffed Clover on the arm. 'Whose friend are you, matey?'

Clover laughed. 'Yours, but I'll be Paige's too.'

'She's teacher's pet as well,' said Tasmin. 'Always sucking up to people.'

'I am so not,' said Clover.

'You are too,' said Tasmin. 'Mum said you'll be going to Queensmead, Paige. We go there. We won't be in the same class but we'll be in the same year. I can show you around a bit.'

Clover nodded. 'I will too. Tell you who to avoid, who's fit etc. There's some decent boy talent in the sixth form, but not many. We prefer college students. They're not so juvenile.'

'Though most boys are,' said Tasmin. 'Whatever age they are.'

'What's the school like?'

Tasmin shrugged. 'Big old boring building.'

'She means what's it like to go there,' said Clover.

'Oh. Usual stuff. Some good teachers, some old farts. Usual mix of people.'

I laughed, then she looked pointedly at what I had on. 'Do you always dress like that?' I felt like saying to her, do *you* always dress like that? Today she was wearing a skimpy tight dress that was way too short.

'I like clothes that are practical I guess—' I started.

'Bo-oring,' said Tasmin. 'You could look really good if you made an effort.'

'And there she goes with her big mouth again,' said Clover. 'Take no notice. Everyone has their own style.'

Tasmin nodded. 'You just haven't found yours yet, have you?'

Clover gave her a look. 'I think you should shut up now, Tas, before you dig yourself in any deeper.'

'It's OK,' I said. 'My friend Allegra often said the same – that I hadn't found my style yet – so I'm not offended.'

Clover got up. 'OK, Paige, so get your lippie on. Tasmin and I are going to take you into town and we can look in some shops and try on some different styles.'

'And show you some of the boy talent in Bath,' added Tasmin.

I didn't like to refuse, seeing as they were being so friendly, and I liked Clover from our short meeting. I obliged by smearing on a bit of lip gloss then set off with the girls to explore my new city.

We caught the bus to the centre of town and, as I gazed out of the window, I began to remember that there was more to Bath than just what was around where Tasmin lived. The bus passed a park and children's playground to our left where I could vaguely remember playing with Tasmin when we were small. We passed a row of terraced houses all with signs advertising B and B outside. Then rows of streets lined with tall, honey-coloured houses began to appear. They looked like something from a period costume drama and I could see more houses with the same stone nestling in woodland on hills to the right behind the town. Very pretty, I thought as we got off the bus opposite an Odeon cinema complex and walked through a square lined with shops and cafés.

Tasmin pointed out a café to our right. 'Good tea and cakes in there.'

There were a number of eateries around the square, some with tables and chairs outside, all occupied with people enjoying the mild weather between the showers. The place had a buzz about it, with a market stall in the middle selling fruit and vegetables, and benches where students sat eating pizza or tortillas from the Mexican restaurant nearby.

'Is this where you hang out?' I asked.

'Sometimes, but we cruise all over. We like to go to McDonald's too,' replied Tasmin. 'Everyone does.'

'We always see someone we know in there,' Clover added. 'And sometimes we hang out on the turf in the middle of the shopping centre. It's paved so no cars go there and there's this fake grass with deck chairs on it in the warm weather. We also like to go up to the Royal Crescent. There's a huge park in front of it and people hang out there too. We'll show you one day.'

'Royal Crescent?' I asked.

Tasmin rolled her eyes. 'Haven't you heard of it? Big curved row of houses at the top of Bath? It's famous. There are loads of other crescents too.'

'Eight in all,' said Clover, 'not loads. She always exaggerates everything.'

'People come from all over the world to see the architecture here,' said Tasmin. 'That's not an exaggeration.'

'Let's take her to the square next to the Abbey,' said Clover as we came into a street lined with shops. 'It's a good place to hang out and listen to live music – someone's always playing there. Take no notice of Tasmin, Paige. Why should you know about the Royal Crescent if you've never lived here?'

'It's not such a bad place to live,' said Tasmin. 'OK yeah, there's all the history stuff but there's a good music scene here, though Bristol is better. Mum and Dad don't like me going there any more though, since I went to a gig with a bunch of mates and didn't get back to Bath til past midnight. They had to pick me up from the train station. I was so in the doghouse that week.'

As we turned into a pedestrianised street, to our right, a woman in her twenties was singing opera in a very wobbly voice. 'God, she warbles,' said Tasmin in a voice loud enough for the street performer to hear. 'I'd like to shoot her.'

Clover sighed. 'Little Miss Subtle with her opinions,' she said.

'I'm beginning to realise,' I replied, though I quite liked Tasmin being so outspoken. I didn't have to worry about what she was thinking because it was out before she could stop herself, so I knew exactly what was going on in her head.

'Take no notice of her. I quite often pretend I'm not with her,' said Clover.

Ahead of us, a bunch of boys and girls were sitting on benches by a hot sausage stall. One of them looked like the boy I'd seen yesterday outside the house. He had his arm around a girl with short chestnut-coloured hair. She wasn't either of the girls I'd seen him with before. He saw me staring so I quickly turned away. He might be good-looking but he was clearly a love rat and I didn't want him thinking I was a contender for his list of conquests. I caught up with Tasmin and Clover and we took a left through some pillars to find there was a huge Abbey in front of us, and an open square to our right.

'Wow, this is *amazing*,' I said as I looked around. The Abbey was an impressive building with enormous wooden doors, and to the left and right of them were tall ladders with statues of people, carved in stone, climbing their way to the top. In front, a crowd was watching a human statue that was sprayed from head to toe in silver paint. He was totally still despite having a pigeon balanced on his hat. A bunch of Japanese tourists took turns having their photo taken with him and even then he didn't move. I took a quick photo on my phone to send to Allegra. To our right was a long line of tourists queuing.

'Where are they going?' I asked.

'The Pump Room or the Roman Baths I guess,' said Clover.

'You get posh tea in the Pump Room,' said Tasmin as we went over and looked through tall windows into what looked like a ballroom. It was filled with tables laid with white cloths and waiters in black-and-white uniforms rushing around carrying silver trays and serving customers. 'The tourists love it.'

I glanced behind me to see if the group of boys and girls by the sausage stand were still there but they'd moved on.

'Er . . . That boy next door to you. Who is he?' I asked.

'Boy next door? To us at home you mean?' Tasmin replied.

I nodded.

'Do you mean to the right? You must because there's only a pair of wrinklies on the left – Mr and Mrs Carson.'

'Yes, to the right.'

'What does he look like?'

'Tall. Brown, medium-length hair. Maybe about eighteen. I only got a glimpse of him.'

'You must mean Niall Peterson. Have you met him already? God, he's fast, but then that's Niall.'

'I haven't met him. I just saw him yesterday when I was looking out the window. What's he like?'

Tasmin raised an eyebrow. 'Don't tell me you fancy him?'

'No way.'

'Good, because he's so full of himself. Thinks he's so cool.'

'You used to think so too Tas,' said Clover.

'Duh. Only about a million years ago. That was back in Year Seven when I didn't know any better. So why do you want to know about him, Paige?'

'Oh no reason,' I said. 'Just wondering who he was, that's all.'

Clover and Tasmin looked at each other. 'She fancies him,' they said in unison.

'I *don't*,' I said. 'I can assure you he is about as far from my type as possible.'

'Yeah right,' they both said in unison.

I could see that protesting was only making things worse, so I decided to give up. They'd realise soon enough I wasn't interested in the creep next door.

'So what is your type?' asked Clover.

I shrugged. 'I . . . I'm not really into boys.'

'You a lezzer?' asked Tasmin. 'It's OK if you are. Susie Railston at our school is and she's one of the coolest girls in our year.'

'No, it's not that. Just . . . I have better things to think about than whether some stupid boy has noticed me or not.'

'Good for you, Paige,' said Clover. 'You're very sensible. Boys mainly do your head in.'

Tasmin looked me up and down. 'Yes. Sensible, that's a good word to describe you.' I knew she was talking about my dress sense as well as anything else. I wished I wasn't. I'd like to be cool and stylish like Clover or a tad wilder like Tasmin, but I didn't want to copy either of them. I wanted to be me, a new me, the real me – but I didn't know who that was. 'But there must have been someone in London? Some secret crush?'

I didn't want to seem straight and boring so decided to tell her about Alex. 'There was one boy. I really liked him. He never noticed me until recently. I'd just got the part of Juliet in the school play and he was going to play Romeo, but it never happened . . . because of the move.'

Tasmin and Clover looked at me sympathetically. 'Oh bummer,' said Clover and she put her arm around me and gave me a squeeze.

'Lezzers,' said Tasmin.

Clover let go of me, pursed her lips and went to kiss Tasmin but she ducked away.

I laughed and it felt good to be with them joshing each other and, for the first time in weeks, I felt myself relax slightly. Maybe it would be all right in Bath after all.

My spirits rose as we made our way further up into the town. There were some of the usual shops you see in every city – Next, BHS, Gap, Office shoes, The Body Shop –but as we went higher up the road and through a narrow lane, there were little boutiques, jewellery shops, all with windows full of knick-knacks, linens, soaps, bath gels. The area was heaving with people looking at the displays, and it was obviously a great place for shopping. I glimpsed a girl with blonde hair ahead of us. She looked exactly like Allegra from the back. I knew it couldn't be her and felt a pang of missing her. *I wish she was here*, I thought. *We could have explored together.*

We walked into the square to the right of the Abbey, which was lined with benches, most occupied by people watching a couple with guitars in the middle. Some people were eating ice creams, others just sitting watching. To our right, I noticed a line of Italian-looking statues high above a wall.

'What's in there?' I asked.

'The Roman Baths,' replied Clover. 'Lots of bits of ancient stones and stuff and a huge pool full of water. It's quite interesting but a bit hot and smelly. Bath water has sulphur in it and smells of bad eggs.'

Tasmin laughed. 'Sell it to her, why don't you?' she said. 'Actually it's interesting in there if you like learning about history.'

We crossed the square, took a left down a narrow street and the area opened up again. Opposite were the green hills I'd seen from the bus and it looked like there were some lovely old houses there, all built in the soft honey-stone that I was beginning to see was typical of the area.

We crossed the road and watched tourists get on a red open-topped, double-decker tourist bus to our right. We leant against a wall and looked below where there was a sunken park and beyond that was a river with a weir. On the opposite bank, a couple of double-decked boats were filling up with more tourists.

'This is a real holiday place, isn't it?' I commented. 'I don't think I ever realised when we visited you before.'

'Understatement,' said Clover. 'The tourists are here all year round.'

'To your left is Pulteney Bridge,' said Tasmin putting on a loud tour-guide type voice, which caused some people to turn and look at her. 'Famous because it has shops on it. Apparently there are only two others like it in the world.'

'One is in Florence,' I said.

'Ooh, get you, clever clogs,' said Tasmin. 'Jane Austen lived here once so the tourists come to see all her hang-out places too, not just the Roman parts. There's even a day when people dress up in clothes from that period and parade around like a bunch of tossers.'

'Seriously?' I asked.

Tasmin nodded. 'It's called the Regency parade. It happens every June. We should make sure we're around this year so we can have a laugh watching everyone.'

'Some of them look mad in the bonnets and the feathers, but those high breeches and long coats look pretty hot on some boys,' said Clover. 'Have you been to Italy, Paige?'

I nodded but didn't elaborate in case she thought I was showing off. I'd been to Venice last year, Tuscany to stay in an old farmhouse the year before, Florence, Sicily, Sardinia, the Amalfi coast and Ravello in years before that. Mum and Dad loved Italy.

'I'm going to go one day,' said Tasmin. 'I want to travel the world.'

I thought it best not to say I'd also been to India, Peru and the Seychelles. We'd had two holidays a year for as long as I could remember. *No more of those either*, I thought as Tasmin and Clover moved off again.

We walked up and down lanes, through an indoor market, then stopped for a cappuccino at a café at the top of the town where there were even more shops and cafés. I couldn't wait to report back to Allegra that first impressions were good. Very good. Bath was buzzing.

Along the way, I learnt that Clover was in a relationship with a boy called Chas who was at Bath Spa University. He was eighteen and a musician who played gigs and earned a fortune busking at the weekends. Tasmin had just broken up with a guy called Stu after three months because 'the spark had gone', though apparently he wanted her back. He was a musician too and played in the same band as Chas. Tasmin had had six boyfriends so far. 'A sl-ut,' said Clover, though none of them sounded that serious or like they'd lasted that long.

Clover seemed to have quite a relationship history too, with four ex-boyfriends, all who'd lasted about four months. I felt inexperienced and naïve as I listened to them talk about boys, school and future plans. Tasmin wasn't sure what she wanted to do when she left school, but a gap year travelling in the Far East was high on the list, and Clover wanted to do something in fashion when she went to college and maybe have her own vintage clothes shop.

'What about you, Paige?' asked Clover.

'I want to study literature or art,' I said, 'though I'm not really sure yet.'

'Literature,' mimicked Tasmin.

'Don't be mean,' said Clover.

Tasmin rolled her eyes. 'Sorry, Paige but you don't half sound posh. Lit-er-a-*ture*.'

I ignored her. I was starting to realise she didn't intend to be mean. She just said what popped into her head. 'Not sure what I'll do with it. Maybe write, but I'm not sure what yet, or paint . . .'

'Write about us,' said Tasmin. 'Can we be in your first novel?'

'Deffo,' I said as we stopped to listen to a boy standing in the middle of the pavement at the top of town. He was playing guitar and singing his heart out.

As we stood there, I noticed a group of teenagers walk past. They stopped on the opposite side to us to watch, although I could see they were more interested in Clover and Tasmin than the singer. I also noticed another boy go to join them.

It was Niall, my new next-door neighbour. He was on his own this time. He listened for a few moments then started heckling the boy, then awoo-howling like a dog. The performer finished his song, glanced at Niall then moved off. *How mean*, I thought and I gave Niall a filthy look. He noticed me looking at him and winked. I rolled my eyes as if to say, 'I am *so* not interested in you'. He clearly didn't get the message because he came over.

'Hey Tas,' he said to my cousin. 'Who's your new friend?'

'Someone *way* out of your league,' said Tasmin. Her phone bleeped that she had a text and she pulled Clover over to look at the message.

Niall turned to me. 'I'm Niall,' he said and gave me what I presume was supposed to be a killer watt smile.

'And *I'm* not interested.'

For a second, hurt registered on his face and I almost regretted my abrupt response. Then I remembered what I'd seen yesterday and today – three girls in under twenty-four hours and him heckling some innocent street performer. He was not a nice guy.

'So you're staying with Tasmin?' he asked.

I nodded and looked away in the hope that he'd go away.

'I saw you looking at me,' he said.

'I was not.'

'You were. In the garden yesterday, then again today by the sausage stall, and if I'm not mistaken you were even spying on me from behind the curtains in Tasmin's bedroom.'

I couldn't believe it. The cheek of him. 'As *if*. I was not spying on you. For your information, I'd just arrived in Bath and was looking out of the window to see where I was.'

Niall put his hand over his heart. 'And then you saw me.'

'Only by accident, I can assure you.'

'So where have you come from?'

'London. Not that it's any of your business. And by the way, I saw you with three different girls, two yesterday and one today. Do they all know about each other?'

Niall raised an eyebrow. 'Excuse me?'

'Three girls in two days?' I repeated.

'Er . . . none of your business,' he said, but his eyes were twinkling as if he found our whole exchange highly amusing. 'So you *were* watching me then?'

'I was *so* not watching you. I told you, I just happened to be looking out of the window.'

'Ah, but maybe that was fate making you look just as I walked by.'

'Pff,' I said and wished I could think of some brilliant put-down.

'So you're a mate of Tasmin's? You don't look like one of her usual crowd.'

He was starting to annoy me. 'And what does her usual crowd look like?' I asked.

'More glamorous.'

Insulting as well as full of himself, I thought. *This boy really is something.* 'Well, your hair needs washing,' I said.

Niall looked shocked. 'Wow. What side of bed did you get out of?'

'You just insulted me saying Tasmin's friends are more glamorous.'

'I didn't mean it in a bad way. You just don't have Tas's loads of make-up, hair-extension look or Clover's vintage queen style—'

'I don't really *care* what you think,' I said.

Niall sighed. I got the feeling that I was starting to annoy him too. *Good*, I thought. *Boys as good-looking as he is think they just have to look at a girl and she falls at his feet. Well, not me.*

He ran the fingers on his left hand through his hair. 'Well at least I can do something about my hair needing washing, whereas you can't change the way you look.'

'That's really rude.'

'And so is telling me my hair needs washing. Actually, I've just been at the gym. It's wet from the shower, that's all.'

'If you say so. Anyway, heckling that guy's singing was really mean.'

Niall's eyes narrowed and I felt as if I had hit a nerve. 'You don't know the whole story there,' he said. 'I guess it looked mean but . . . we have history.'

'Like what? Tell me? I'd like to understand why you scared some kid off, then snogged three girls in less than twenty-four hours, and *then* insulted me.'

Niall sighed. 'I didn't snog three girls . . . er . . . only two. Look. I came over to be friendly. Clearly not a good idea. OK, just forget it. I think I'll be going now.'

'*Me* too,' I said.

Niall turned to go, then turned back. 'Just one thing before I go, Miss Judgemental. What you see isn't always what's going on.'

'Meaning?'

'Don't make judgements until you know all the facts.'

'You mean like what I saw with my own two eyes?'

A look of exasperation flashed across Niall's face. 'I give up. You're obviously one of those stuck-up girls who thinks you know it all.'

'And you're obviously one of those boys who's full of himself, insensitive and mean.'

I suddenly realised that Tasmin and Clover had finished on the phone and were listening in.

'Ah love at first sight,' said Tasmin.

'As *if*,' chorused Niall and I.

I turned and walked away. I couldn't stand another minute with him. He was *so* annoying. Clover and Tasmin ran to catch me up as I hurried down the pavement. I'd never had such a horrible conversation with anyone, ever, and it had upset me.

'Hey, slow down,' said Clover. 'Tasmin was only teasing and so probably was Niall.'

'He's such a creep,' I said.

'So don't let him get to you,' said Tasmin. 'He loves winding girls up. He thinks it's big. Don't react. That's what he wants.'

I nodded. I felt cross with him and cross with myself for giving my feelings away. *There's a good reason I'm so reserved usually – the less people know about what's going on inside of me, the less they can be horrible*, I thought.

Clover linked one arm and Tasmin the other. 'Come on, let's go home and listen to music. Not all boys are like Niall, Paige. Honestly there are some really nice ones in Bath.'

'And we just happen to know most of them,' said Clover.

They were doing their best to make me feel better

but it was too late. I felt exposed and insecure. *One thing I do know for certain though*, I told myself, *and that is that I'm going to avoid Niall Peterson for the rest of my time in Bath.*

Later that day, Tasmin went off to Clover's house. I didn't want to outstay my welcome and be a Miss Tag-Along so I went home and up to my bedroom. I noticed the *Songs for Sarah* CD lying where Tasmin had left it on her chest of drawers. I put it in the player and lay back on the bed to listen.

> Sometimes on a crowded street, I see someone
>   just like you.
> I want to call out, 'Hey, hello,' though I know it
>   can't be so.
> You're far away, my lovely friend, the space
>   between us never ends.

Allegra. She was my far-away friend. The words of the song brought tears to my eyes.

Chapter Nine

New school. New nightmare. April the eighth. It was a day I'd been dreading ever since I'd heard that I'd be changing schools, though part of me had blocked it out as far as I could because I knew it wasn't going to be easy.

Tasmin and I got up the next morning, had breakfast, then got a lift with Uncle Mike who teaches music at the same school. Tasmin was in the black-and-white uniform of the school with her skirt hoiked short as usual. I'd been told I was OK to wear my own clothes until I got the uniform but I'd dressed in a pair of black trousers and white shirt so that I didn't stand out as the newbie too much.

I felt removed from what was going on like it was happening to someone else and any moment I'd snap out of the numb state of mind I was in, wake up and things would be back to normal. The last few weeks would all have been a bad dream. As I sat in the back of the car and looked out of the window at the cars and buses filled with pupils heading for the same school, I felt my stomach churn with anxiety.

Once we'd arrived at Queensmead and Uncle Mike had dropped us off at the front, we saw Clover waiting for us at the tall glass door leading to reception. Even in school uniform, she managed to look cool with her hair pulled back flat on top of her head and rolled up at the back in a nineteen-fifties type bun. The style suited her and highlighted her lovely heart-shaped face. She linked arms with me. 'You OK?' she asked.

'Not sure,' I replied as we followed Tasmin inside. Changing school was not part of how I'd seen my year unfolding back on December the thirty-first when Allegra and I had made our new year's resolutions and talked over our plans, but there was no going back. It felt like someone had a very firm hand in the small of my back and was propelling me into this new and unfamiliar chapter.

I also felt that I couldn't really talk to anyone about it, and that was difficult too. I definitely couldn't open up to Mum and Dad. They were struggling with their own adjustment and I didn't want to add to their worry. Tasmin and Clover had been kind and sympathetic and, because of that, I didn't feel I could open up to them either. They might think I thought I was too good for their school or that I was always miserable, and so not want to spend any time with me. I didn't want to blow the beginning of the only friendships I had so far. The only person I'd confided in was Allegra and she'd sent me a text early in the morning with three kisses. It was sweet of her but hearing from her only reminded me that she was on her own way into school, the school back in London where I belonged and knew my way around.

'It will be fine,' said Tasmin, as if picking up on my thoughts. 'Most people are OK here. Come on, we'll do a quick tour and show you where everything is before lessons.'

We pushed our way through corridors busy with pupils bustling and hustling to get past each other, greeting friends, getting to the hall or a classroom. A cacophony of adolescent voices made the noise level almost unbearable and I struggled to hear anything Tasmin or Clover said to me as they pointed out various landmarks – the library, the loos, the main hall, the canteen. Tasmin had told me that there were one and a half thousand pupils at this school. There had been four hundred at my old one.

We finally got to the common room for Year Ten and Eleven where the mania ceased. It was quiet at last when Clover shut a door behind us. My first impression was that the room smelt of Pot Noodles. A number of pupils were already in there, some seated. A group of girls were making tea at a kettle by a sink in the left corner, others were catching up with gossip from the holidays, judging by the shrieks of laughter. 'And then what did he do?' I heard one of them ask. A dark-haired boy was absorbed in his laptop near the window, another couple were sitting in the corner chatting. All of them looked up when we walked in, curious glances checking me out. I wanted to slope away and observe from a corner but Tasmin pointed to me and said in a loud voice, 'New girl alert. Name of Paige Lord. My cousin. Be nice or else.'

The girls at the kettle gave me a weary wave then turned back to their drinks and chat. The boys went back to what they were doing. Clearly, I wasn't worthy of any more interest.

Tasmin and Clover were soon busy catching up

with the girls at the kettle and I grabbed a seat to take in the new environment – tall windows in need of a good clean to the left, noticeboard with various posters to the right, lockers at the far end, and rows of well-worn brown fabric chairs arranged to make benches along the middle and back of the room. Inside me a battle was taking place.

One part of me felt about five years old, overwhelmed, bewildered and finding it hard to breathe when I thought about how so much had changed so fast. If I gave in to that side of me, I knew I would curl up and cry. Another stronger part of me was telling me that I must be brave, remind myself of what was good in my life, everything Mr Nash, my old headmaster, used to lecture us about in past school assemblies and we used to laugh about later. Now I needed all the positivity he preached and I mentally ran the checklist of things to be grateful for that he used to read out to us. *I have my health, I have my intellect, I have potential friends, I have a roof over my head even if it's not my own. I have food to eat. I have clothes to wear.*

It didn't wash. A third part of me wanted to tell Mr Nash to go and stuff himself because what had happened to me and Mum and Dad felt grossly, horribly unfair and I didn't want to be there in this strange school with one and a half thousand unfamiliar faces.

'Paige,' said a voice next to me.

I looked up to see a blond boy standing in front of me. He looked familiar. He was one of the musicians I'd seen in the café when I'd gone to find Mum on Saturday.

'Oh hi, yes, I'm Paige. How do you know my name?' I asked.

He pointed to the other side of the common room, which was now filling up with more and more people. 'Tasmin. She's telling everyone to come and say hello.'

I rolled my eyes. 'How embarrassing.'

The boy nodded. 'She means well. I'm Liam. You've just moved here from London?'

'Is there anything she didn't tell you?' I asked.

Liam smiled. 'A lot. So, first day. How are you feeling?'

'Fine. No. That's a lie. I feel slightly insane, like there are all these different parts of me inside doing battle. Voices all saying something different.' I don't normally blurt out my inner feelings to strangers but I was feeling so nervous and out of place, I couldn't stop myself. I was hoping Liam would nod and tell me that he felt like that some days too. But he didn't. He looked slightly alarmed and stared at me as if he didn't get what I was saying at all. 'You hear voices?'

'No! Not exactly voices, that sounds mad, just I . . . ' I blustered. 'I was just feeling . . . oh never mind.'

Liam glanced at his watch then heaved his rucksack over his shoulder. 'OK. Better get going. Um. Guess I'll see you around, Paige. Welcome to Bath and er . . . good luck with the voices.'

Well that went well for a first encounter, not, I thought as Tasmin beckoned me to get up and go and join her. 'Come on,' she said. 'Lesson time. We'll deliver you to your classroom then see you back here at lunch, OK?'

I gave her a quick hug. 'I really appreciate what you're trying to do, Tasmin. It's very generous of you, especially after I've taken up half your room and everything.' I felt like I was about to cry. Tasmin saw it too.

She returned my hug. 'Hey, stupid. Don't go all wussy on me. I don't do soppy.'

I sniffed back the tears. 'Sorry. I won't.'

Tasmin looked at me with a serious expression. 'I mean it. You've got to tough this out.'

I nodded and Tasmin gave my arm a squeeze. *She has a good heart*, I thought, then felt myself getting tearful again when I considered how I'd disrupted her life and yet she'd come round so quickly. I wasn't sure I could have been that generous. I took a deep breath. *A day at a time*, I told myself. *Just get through a day at a time*.

I did get through the day. And the next. And the week. And the next. Uncle Mike took Dad, Mum and I out in the car a few times after school and at the weekends. He drove us through the city, showed us the famous crescents and the five-storey Georgian houses there, up the steep hills to the outer areas around the rim, then out to picturesque villages and pubs only ten minutes away in the country. We glimpsed some beautiful old manor houses on the edge of the city, nestling amongst trees in private grounds. I think they were hard for Mum and Dad to see because they were so like our old home back in Richmond. To begin with, I couldn't remember which part was where, but slowly, over the weeks, parts of it began to be familiar, particularly the area where we lived and the centre of town.

At school, Tasmin and Clover did their best to look

out for me but, despite their good intentions, I was still the new girl and I was often on my own. Starting a new school after Year Seven is difficult at any time because all the friendships and cliques get established in the first terms when everyone arrives together from junior school, and then they carry on through the following years. By Year Ten the bonds are fixed and any newbie stands out like a sore thumb. People were friendly enough to me but no one went out of their way to ask me to hang out or join their group. They asked a few questions – Where was I from? Why had I moved to Bath? – but they soon left me to myself. They had their own friends to talk to.

I tried to join the drama group, thinking that would be a good way to meet new people, but they were midway through a production so I'd missed the boat there. My one refuge was the art room, where I spent at much time as I could. I'd started a project on portraits at my last school and took photos of Tasmin and Clover to paint, but it was a solitary activity because the art teacher insisted on no talking when working, even if after school.

I sorely missed having Allegra to go home with and to gossip about the day over tea and toast, to have those conversations that were so easy with her and that went from the sublime to the ridiculous and back again in the space of five minutes. We Skyped most evenings and did our best to maintain the closeness we'd always had, but although what was happening at my old school was of interest to me, my new school wasn't of the same interest to her, apart from whether there were any decent boys or not. Not that she didn't ask about my new life – she did, but it wasn't the same as talking about people we both knew.

My life felt uneventful. I went to school in the morning, kept my head down and soon slotted into the syllabus. I was happy to work hard because it gave me something to do. I particularly liked my art teacher, so that was at least something. I did my homework, I ate my packed lunch, then went to the library or art room. I did all the study that was needed, then I went home, often on my own because I couldn't follow Tasmin around like a lap dog, although she always invited me to go and hang out with her and Clover. She had her life and I was already taking up enough of it by living in her bedroom. I wanted to give her space.

I knew I wasn't being totally honest with Allegra when she asked how things were, but I didn't want to alienate her either by letting her know that I was sad, lonely, angry and frustrated. What could she do to change things? Nothing. So I put on my cheery Paige face, making the best of it. Bath is great. School is fine. I'm OK. I'm tough, a survivor. But it was all an act. Inside, I longed for someone to see beyond my mask, to understand how I really felt and to reach out and rescue me.

One evening after I'd Skyped Allegra, I put on the *Songs for Sarah* CD. I stood and looked out of the window as a soundtrack filled the room.

> Put a frame around my face,
> Hang it in a gallery,
> So perfectly proportioned,
> Don't you wish you looked like me?
> But when I look in the mirror,
> Who is it that I see?
> Someone who's sad and lonely,
> Could this be the real me?

Spooky. That's just how I've been feeling today, I thought, when I heard Aunt Karen call that supper was ready. The more I listened to the CD, the more

the songs spoke to me. I'd got into the habit of playing a track every evening when I got home from
school if Tasmin wasn't in. I even copied the CD onto
my iPod so that I could listen during the day. It was
weird, like every track I put on seemed to echo my
life. I thought of it as a playlist for my broken heart
because it always made me feel better and less alone.
I wonder who made it and where he is? I asked myself as
I switched off the player, then went down the stairs to
join the mayhem that was supper time with my cousins. An idea suddenly hit me. Maybe I could look for
him?

'Where's Dad?' I asked Mum after we'd eaten and
were alone in the kitchen filling the dishwasher. He
wasn't around most days for mealtimes and I was
beginning to miss him.

'Out looking to get our lives back,' said Mum as
she cleared uneaten food into the bin. I'd pressed her
a few times about when we might get a place of our
own but she was always vague and said that Dad was
doing what he could, checking out possibilities. She
seemed a bit down whenever we spoke about the
future because Dad had been for a few interviews for
jobs but was told each time that he was overqualified.

Mum was luckier and had got a job working in the office at the school on the other side of town where Aunt Karen worked as an art teacher. Someone was on maternity leave so everyone at the school was super grateful to Mum and she seemed to be happy to have something to do and somewhere to go in the mornings.

'And are you OK working at the school?' I asked.

'It will do for now,' she replied. She always said that. For now, but how long would that be?

'What about your degree?' I asked. 'Couldn't you use that to do something you might really enjoy?' Mum had been to the London College of Fashion when she'd left school and done a course in costume design. She'd wanted to work in theatre but then she met Dad and her life became looking after him, the house and then me.

'Maybe,' she replied. 'But I have no CV. "Housewife" doesn't count for much.'

'But what about all the charity events you worked on? You have amazing organisational skills.'

Mum sighed. 'Maybe one day I'll use those skills again. In the meantime, the job I have is a godsend. It's giving me a chance to catch my breath while your dad and I rethink the plan.'

I gave her a hug. She was putting on her cheery Mum face just as I was putting on my cheery Paige one. I sometimes wondered if the whole world wasn't going around hiding behind masks.

As we put dishes away, out of the window I noticed that someone had gone into next-door's garden. It was Niall. On seeing him, I felt a pang of regret that our last encounter had gone so badly. I hated there to be bad feeling with anyone, even if he was a love rat. Despite my early vow to avoid him, I decided to go and try to make amends, so when Mum made a cup of coffee and went through to the living room, I took a deep breath, opened the back door and went out.

There was a fence with lattice on the top to the right of the garden but I could see him clearly through it. I went over and called, 'Hi.'

He almost jumped out of his skin, which made me laugh.

'Sorry,' I said. 'I didn't mean to startle you.'

'What are you doing? Lurking in the bushes?'

'No. Not lurking. I . . . I saw you and wanted to apologise for the other day. I guess I wasn't very friendly.'

A glimmer of a smile crossed Niall's face. 'No. I guess not. But maybe I'm like Marmite. You either love me or hate me.'

'I like Marmite,' I said.

Niall grinned. 'Me too, so at least we have something in common.'

I felt myself blush and cursed in case he'd noticed. I didn't want him to think that meant that I liked him.

'At least sometimes I do . . . I . . . no, I'm probably more in the middle when it comes to Marmite, I don't love it or hate it. I'm . . . indifferent.' I realised that I was rambling. *Shut up*, I told myself when I noticed the amused look in Niall's eye. *He'll think you're an idiot.*

'So, you're going to Queensmead?' he asked.

'Yes. How do you know?'

'Seen you leave the house with Tasmin.'

'Oh, been watching me out the window have you?' I asked, echoing what he had asked me when I met him in town, then I worried that I might have sounded hostile again.

'Not watching, but I've seen you a few times. Can't help but notice people on the street, can you?'

'Exactly,' I said and even I could tell I sounded prissy.

Niall's mobile rang and he pulled it out of his pocket. 'Got to take this,' he said.

'Probably one of your girlfriends,' I blurted before I could stop myself.

Niall shook his head as if he couldn't believe what I'd said. He turned away to take his call and I darted back into the house.

Stupid, stupid, I told myself as I went upstairs. I am so hopeless at talking to boys. Why can't I be cool like Clover or confident like Tasmin? Instead I come across as someone with a permanent case of PMT. It's like there's a part of me that's been held back and is fighting to get out, but when she does get out, what she says is wrong, wrong, wrong.

Chapter Ten

One evening in my fourth week at Queensmead, I got back to Aunt Karen's and went up to Tasmin's room as usual. Tasmin had gone into town to watch a new romcom so I had the bedroom to myself.

I'd decided I was going to take the series of portraits I'd been working on in London a stage further and develop the faces into masks. I did some research online about different masks and got completely immersed for an hour or so as images from around the world filled the screen. I found ancient masks as old as nine thousand years, masks from different countries, some grotesque, some beautiful. I loved the ones from Venice that I'd seen when I was there for the carnival with Mum and Dad a few years ago. I made some sketches and was about to Skype Allegra when I got a text from her saying that she was going to see the same movie as Tasmin and Clover and that she'd call later.

I lay back on the bed and stared at the ceiling for a while but all the angst I was feeling inside immediately came to the fore. Why has this all happened to us? When will we get our own place? Will I ever fit in at the new school? Will Mum and Dad be OK? I couldn't relax. Luckily Mum called that supper was ready.

I went downstairs to find the usual pandemonium that was Aunt Karen's house at mealtime. It was a far cry from the quiet suppers I used to have with Mum back in Richmond when Dad came home late most weekday evenings. She'd always have something light. She didn't do carbs after midday so it was grilled chicken or fish and salad or steamed vegetables. I'd sometimes have the same, or pasta.

At Aunt Karen's, there was always a big pot of something like chicken casserole and vegetables or chilli, or a pasta bake from the oven, that was put in the centre of the table and ladled out into bowls, then eaten with baked potatoes or rice with grated cheese and huge chunks of wholemeal bread. I noticed that as the days went on that Mum was letting go of the no carbs rule and helped herself to rice or potatoes along with everyone else. Jo, Jake and Simon all talked over each other to get their mother's attention, particularly Jake, who raised the volume of any sentence towards the end of what he was saying in order to drown out which ever other brother was attempting to get a word in.

Tasmin was often not there at mealtimes and if she was, she ate then ran, always busy seeing Clover or friends. I didn't feel as though I could do that without appearing rude. Uncle Mike liked to have music – country blues – on in the background and he seemed to manage to screen out his sons' competing voices and listen to the CDs. Dad still absented himself from these meals saying that he preferred to eat later. I knew he couldn't handle the noise level either. I often caught Mum watching me across the dining table. She'd smile at me sympathetically. She knew that I found it hard too.

After supper, I always made sure that I helped with the clearing up. I didn't want Aunt Karen or Uncle Mike to think that I took anything for granted. The boys were good at mucking in too. Aunt Karen had them well trained and, as the adults took their coffees into the sitting room to watch the news, Jo and Jake stacked the dishwasher then disappeared fast to play their computer games. I wiped the surfaces down then went to put out the rubbish for the bin men in the morning.

When I reached the street, I saw Niall was also putting out rubbish. I was about to turn back but it was too late – he was bound to have seen me. I tried to think up something funny to say about the bins but he turned away before I got a chance to say anything. I knew he'd seen me just as clearly as I'd seen him. *I must have really annoyed him when I saw him in the garden but he could have at least said hi*, I thought as I went back inside, where the noise levels seemed to have grown.

The TV was on in the sitting room, Uncle Mike had moved into the kitchen and was playing his guitar along to a soundtrack, and Aunt Karen was talking to someone on the phone – or rather shouting to make herself heard over the din. I went through and watched a bit of TV but the boys wanted to watch the cartoon channel, which I found boring after a while. Plus, it was hard to concentrate with Mum and Aunt Karen chatting away in the background and Simon on some very annoying and loud PlayStation game. I didn't blame Dad for making himself scarce. I went back upstairs to read. *One day I will have my own life*, I told myself. I had my plan. Get my GCSEs, do A levels, apply for uni in London, move back to my home ground and share a flat with Allegra and have some *space*.

When I got back up to the room, I decided to tidy up my half. I didn't dare touch Tasmin's stuff though it drove me mad the way she left everything out and never ever closed drawers. *Still, it's her room, she can do what she likes*, I reminded myself. I found my iPod, put my earphones in and pressed play as I put a few books into a pile. The first track began to play. *Great*, I thought as Aunt Karen's house, and the noise within it, receded to be replaced by a ballad accompanied by piano. It was one of my favourite tracks so far.

> All alone yet so many voices in my head,
> removed from my life, may as well be half dead.
> I'm in a dream, in a haze,
> looking for love, a way out of this daze.
> Where is the life I knew? Those sun-filled rooms?
> Once so full of hope, now I see cobwebs, remind-
>   ers of how things used to be.

There was a break for the piano. The whole piece was poignant, full of sadness and longing. Like so many of the other tracks, it really spoke to me. The words articulated my experience exactly. Every track on the CD expressed different feelings but mainly seemed to be about someone searching for love, searching for who they were. I could relate to them all.

The more I'd listened to the CD over the weeks since I'd got it, I began to think that whoever had made it was telling a story through the tracks that they'd chosen. The progression of a love affair from loneliness to first attraction, a girl who stood out from the crowd, someone special, hope, dreams of how things might be. The later tracks were full of hope, reaching out to a soulmate. What happened? Did he find her? *And can I find him?* I asked myself as I took out my earphones, picked up the CD case from by the bed and examined the cover.

It was definitely homemade and, as I studied it, I could make out how it had been created. It was a paper collage of two, maybe three, pages from a magazine. I looked more closely. Two pages. The top page had been ripped up in strips then stuck down vertically on top of the page beneath, leaving gaps a couple of centimetres apart so you could see through to the image below as if looking through bars. On the top page, I could make out an abstract image of a girl in four colours: red, black, brown and a flesh tone. In the top right, there was an upturned face in profile, the eye heavily made up. The face was large in proportion to the rest of the body, which was shown in the bottom right. I could make out a red skirt, a leg with a green high heel.

As I stared at the image, it became clearer. The body was falling away to the bottom right. In the centre was a black mark, which could represent hair but as I looked closer, I realised it was a crotchet from a music score. I focused on the image that had been placed underneath and that could be seen through the gaps between the torn strips on top. It was a photograph in browns and blues and was harder to make out than the top ripped page. To the right, I could see a boy's head, taken from high above. Brown hair, an eyebrow, a nose, to the left a jean-clad hip and leg. In the centre, his hand over a . . . what was it? Maybe a guitar? As I refocused on both images, I saw that they had been placed so that the boy's head appeared to be in the girl's mind. *Clever*, I thought as I turned the CD case over.

On the back was a black-and-white photograph. I had glanced at it when I'd seen it in the charity shop but hadn't looked at it properly since. It was a figure, a boy by a window looking out on a building opposite – red brick not Bath stone, I could tell that much. Above was clear sky. I screwed my eyes up to see if I could make out the boy's face. I couldn't. His features were dark because he was in silhouette against the window, buildings and sky behind him. I couldn't tell if he was facing the camera or turned away. I was more intrigued than ever. Who was this boy? I'd really like to find him. Talk to him. Find out what the story was. Why he'd made the CD and why it ended up in a box of jumble in a charity shop. I got up to look for my pencil case. When I found it, I pulled out my magnifying glass. I'd just gone back to studying the photograph when Tasmin and Clover walked in.

Clover sat next to me and I could smell that she'd been drinking alcohol. 'What you doing?'

Tasmin sat on her bed opposite Clover and I and glanced at the CD case in my hand. 'Been listening to some music?'

Clover took the case out of my hand. 'What is it?'

'That CD that Aunt Karen bought for me from the charity shop near here.'

'Oh yeah, there were some good tracks as I remember,' said Tasmin.

'Yes, it's really good, although I don't recognise any

of the tracks,' I replied. 'From the case, it looks like a homemade compilation.' I didn't elaborate on how the music had made me feel in case they asked why I felt they spoke to me. I would have felt too exposed if I revealed how lost I was at the moment.

Clover was examining the CD case and opened it. 'There's a list of the tracks and the bands on the inside sleeve.'

Tasmin leant forward. 'Let's have a look.'

She got up and took the CD case from Clover and scrutinised the list inside. I could smell that she'd been drinking alcohol too, but didn't say anything in case they told me that it was none of my business. 'I know some of these bands, most of them in fact. They're local.'

Local? I thought. *In that case, the boy who made the CD probably is as well.*

'Let's have a listen then,' said Clover.

I didn't admit that I had the music on my iPod because it was my private refuge from the world and I didn't want to talk about that. However, Tasmin took the CD out of the case, put it in the CD player and pressed play. A soundtrack filled the room. The girls lay back, Clover on my bed, so we were top and tail, and Tasmin on hers.

So now your world is broken and dark clouds fill
    the air,
And you're living in the shadows, full of sadness,
    doubt and fear.
There's a light that shines within you, it gets
    brighter as you learn
That happiness isn't given, it's something that is
    earned.
Take a look around you, find the one among a
    crowd
And though you've never met him, you'll call his
    name out loud

'Bit gloomy in the beginning,' said Tasmin when the track had finished and she clicked the CD off. I didn't think so. I loved the lyrics and the sentiment that somewhere out there might be someone who could rescue you from the shadows.

Clover picked up the CD case. 'I know this band,' she said. 'They're called Overheated. They're a Bristol band. I've heard them play. Some of the others are from here in Bath though.'

'Do you think that whoever made it lives here in Bath?' I asked.

'Maybe, and if not, they live somewhere nearby,'

said Tasmin. She took the case from Clover and looked at the photo on the back. 'The buildings on the photo on the back don't look like Bath, though it could be – there are a lot of new builds here as well as all the ancient buildings. Do you think it's him on the back, the boy who made it?'

'I was wondering,' I said.

Tasmin picked up my magnifying glass and, just as I had, scrutinised the CD case, then Clover did the same.

'A mystery,' said Clover as she screwed her eyes up trying to see the boy's face.

'A mystery boy,' said Tasmin. 'I like a mystery.'

'I know this might sound mad,' I said, 'but I'd like to try and find him.'

Clover and Tasmin looked at each other then Tasmin nodded.

'Could be fun,' she said.

'Yeah, I'm in,' said Clover.

The quest to find the mystery boy begins, I thought. *Excellent.*

Chapter Eleven

Mystery Boy

'A heart to love, and in that heart
Courage to make's love known.'
                Shakespeare: *Macbeth* – Act 2, Scene 3.

I finished the CD last week and spent the weekend making a cover. I wanted to make something that would stand out. Not a heart. Way too soppy. Not flowers. My girl deserves something unique. A piece of art with a message hidden for her to find. A message that also says I'd noticed her and saw that she was different. I'd leave clues in the artwork so she can track me down. Will she get them? Or will I have to reveal myself to her later?

I tried many designs and one almost worked but I wanted something of me to be in it as well. I was flipping through a magazine when I saw it. A painting of a girl, just about the right size for a CD cover. It looked like she was floating in the air, her face upturned, her body falling away beneath her. *I'll make a collage*, I thought. *That will work.*

I ripped the page from the magazine into four strips. I put a photo of me down first then stuck strips of the ripped page on top like prison bars. Through the bars, she'd be able to see part of me but not enough that she'd recognise me. I wanted her to listen to the tracks, get to know me and how I feel through them as well as relate to them herself. I also wanted her to know that I am someone who knows she's special. On the back of the CD case, I put a black-and-white photo of myself, silhouetted against the window, my face in shadow.

I hoped she'd be intrigued.

Chapter Twelve

'Alex Taylor said to say hi,' said Allegra when we had our Skype catch-up later that evening. Tasmin had gone over to Clover's house so I'd been left on my own again. I could have gone with her but I wanted to talk to Allegra and then start my search for the mystery boy by looking on the internet for some of the bands on the *Songs for Sarah* playlist. I couldn't stop thinking about the music and the boy who had made it because, as well as the tracks expressing how I'd been feeling lately, I got this strange sensation that I was meant to find the CD. I'm not normally fatalistic. I believe you have to make things happen in your life but I felt it was somehow meant for me.

'Paige, are you listening?' said Allegra.

'Yes. Wow. Alex Taylor? To me?' I felt my heart flutter at the mention of his name.

'Yeah, course to you, dummy. And there's more. He said he has a cousin or some relative near Bath and maybe you could meet up next time he's there.' Allegra grinned out at me from the screen.

All thoughts about the CD melted away in the light of this news. 'Me? No way!' Alex here in Bath? That would be amazing. 'He did say something about having lived here before London and that he sometimes comes back but I didn't think he really meant it.' My mind was off already imagining his visit. I could meet him in Society Café that Tasmin had shown me in Kingsmead Square.

'Good hey? I think he's interested because he asked a bit about you – how you're getting on down here and stuff. I've been asking around about him too and he is currently unattached.'

'But he must have a million girls after him.'

'So? Doesn't mean he didn't notice you. You're a very striking girl.' Allegra said the last sentence in the posh voice of her mother. Course my doubt about Alex being interested in me set Allegra off on one of her 'have more confidence in yourself' lectures. Allegra was always Miss Popular with the boys. Not me though, which is why I lack confidence. My boy experience was zilch apart from the time Simon Martin got drunk at a Christmas party and tried to snog me in the conservatory. It was disgusting. His breath was sour from beer and he threw up over a pot plant five minutes later. It was my first kiss – not exactly the stuff of romance to cherish forever. Secretly I felt anxious about kissing and wondered if I'd be any good at it when I met someone I actually liked.

I felt on a high when I ended the call with Allegra. Alex Taylor maybe coming to Bath and he wants to meet up with me! I went on to Facebook to remind myself of his handsome face. *Ohmigod*, I thought as I found my page. There was a friend request from him. I quickly clicked confirm and, moments later, I was able to look at his page and his photos. Album after album: his skiing holiday; him by a pool with a bunch of mates, loads of him with various girls. Just scrolling through them brought back all the feelings I had for him. He was The One. I was sure of it.

The only part of his page that I didn't like was reading about the rehearsals for the school play. However, I told myself, if he'd have fallen in love with the new Juliet, he wouldn't be thinking about hooking up with a girl in Bath, would he? That thought made me feel better and after twenty minutes, I tore myself away and began looking on the net for bands on the *Songs for Sarah* playlist, but some of my earlier enthusiasm had gone. I felt confused. I wanted to find the mystery boy because his music had given me comfort, especially in my earliest days in Bath, and the tracks had made me feel that I wasn't so alone and I was intrigued by it all. But now I knew that Alex Taylor was coming to Bath and maybe Allegra too, did it really matter about meeting the boy who made the CD any more? I decided to have a look online anyway and started by typing in the first band on the list. Sainted.

A few links came up but, from what I could make out, they were out of date – and then there was a post saying that the band had split up about three months ago. Next I typed in Black Pearl. There were loads of links for them so I pressed on the first. It said that they were playing at the market on Walcot Street in Bath. I checked the date to see if the post was an old one too but no, they were playing *this* Saturday. I knew I had homework to do but I was hooked. I had to see if I could learn anything from any of the other bands.

For the next half-hour, I went through the list and discovered that most of the bands had Facebook pages. All of them posted where they were playing next. I also realised that, apart from Sainted, the bands were current – which meant that the CD was probably not made too long ago.

When Tasmin appeared, I was buzzing with energy. I found the page on my computer about Black Pearl's gig on Friday and filled her in on what I'd discovered so far.

'We have to go,' she said as she read the page. 'Looks like it might be some kind of music festival. They often have them there.'

'Cool. And we already know that Mystery Boy likes the band, which is why he chose one of their tracks. Wow, Tasmin, he might be there at the gig.'

'He might. But how are we supposed to recognise him?' she asked.

I wasn't going to be put off. I tapped the side of my nose. 'Follow the clues.'

Tasmin laughed. 'You haven't changed at all,' she said. 'I remember when we were little you used to love mystery games. Remember that Easter when Mum did an Easter egg hunt in the garden? We were about seven. You loved it and found the most. I was so jealous but you shared them with me.'

I vaguely remembered Tasmin with her face covered with chocolate. She was right, I did used to like playing hide and seek or any game that involved having to find something or someone.

'So do you think this mystery boy might be the love of your life then?' asked Tasmin as she lay back on her bed.

I thought about Alex and shook my head as I made a note of the time for Black Pearl's performance on Saturday. 'No. I'd like to know who he is but I want to find out more about the story. Who was Sarah and what happened? She might have chucked the CD out after dumping him. From the music, it sounds like the boy was searching for himself as much as for her. He sounds very romantic. He might have been too much for her but his expectations were too high. Who knows? It's intriguing, isn't it?'

I glanced over at Tasmin. She was fast asleep.

Chapter Thirteen

Mystery Boy

'The course of true love never did run smooth.'
Shakespeare: A Midsummer Night's Dream
– Act 1, Scene 1.

Wednesday night. I go to the park on the way home from school with the CD. I know the time she comes through with her dog now. His name is Geoffrey. I've learnt that much because I've heard her call his name. How can I get the CD to her? I can't just walk up and hand it to her. I want her to listen to it. I want it to speak to her heart the way she has spoken to mine. I want her to think, *Oh, I'd like to know who put this together*. I could follow her home, find out her address and post it. But that would seem like I was stalking her and I'm not a creep, and I don't want her to think of me as one. How could I make it romantic? Hire a flock of birds to carry it to her? No chance. The only birds in the park are pigeons and I wouldn't want them pooping on her head.

I stood under a tree for almost an hour. No sign of her – and then the heavens opened. I got soaked to the skin.

Thursday: back to the park. I see Geoffrey. She can't be far behind him. My heart begins to pound as I anticipate giving her the CD. I could stroll past her, say, 'I think you dropped this.' But then she'd see me. What to do? She's getting closer. My heart beats faster. Noooo. She's with three of her mates. I turn away.

Friday: back in the park. I see a bunch of kids playing, their parents some distance off. I call one of them over, give him a quid and tell him to give the envelope to the lady who'll come by in a minute with a dog. He agrees and goes off. I stand behind my tree, watch and wait. The boy's father is talking to him. He looks at the envelope. Looks over to my tree. I retreat behind it before he sees me. The father looks annoyed and puts the CD in the litter bin. The boy gets a telling off. His father takes him by the hand and marches him out of the park. My girl comes, Geoffrey pulling her ahead as always.

I wait until she's gone, go to the bin and retrieve my love songs.

Bummer. Getting it to her will have to wait until another day.

Chapter Fourteen

'We have some news,' said Dad at the breakfast table on Friday morning. It was the tenth of May and we'd been in Bath five weeks. 'I think we've found a flat.' I knew that this might be a possibility but hadn't wanted to get my hopes up too much. I knew that Dad had been looking at properties for rent in the area since the moment we'd got to Bath, but he'd had no luck because all the rental agencies wanted details of bank accounts and income, neither of which he could provide any more.

Mum said he'd been getting depressed about it until he met an old friend of Uncle Mike's who'd come up with a solution. He had a flat on the south side of Bath that he rented out and his tenants were about to leave. Uncle Mike had filled his friend in on the bare bones of our story, assured him that we would keep up payments and that Uncle Mike would stand as our guarantor. His friend had agreed to give it three months with an option to continue after that if there were no problems.

Dad turned to me. 'So you want to come and take a look tomorrow morning? I can get the keys today.'

I glanced over at Tasmin who gave her head a small shake as if to say, 'No'. She couldn't speak because she had her mouth full of Coco Pops. We had our plan to meet up with Clover and then go to the music festival on Walcot Street. I was really looking forward to it but I didn't want to let Dad down either. He appeared so much better than in recent weeks and seemed to have got some of his old sparkle back.

'Yes, course I do,' I replied, avoiding Tasmin's glare at my answer. I wanted to go to the festival but I also wanted to see where we might be living. 'Then I'm going into town if that's OK.'

'Of course it is. We won't be long. We just wanted to show you the place,' said Mum. 'We've already seen it and . . . well, it isn't our old home in Richmond, but it will be our own space again.'

121

Everyone will be glad of that, I thought as I looked around the kitchen, which was cluttered with the debris from nine people having breakfast.

'Amen to that,' said Tasmin as if reading my thoughts. 'No offence meant.'

'None taken,' I said as I helped myself to some raspberry yoghurt.

On Saturday morning, Dad showed me around our new home. It was the first-floor flat in a four-storey Georgian terraced house in a small square on the other side of Bath to Aunt Karen's – two bedrooms, kitchen-diner, bathroom and large elegant sitting room with tall windows that overlooked the square below. It was unfurnished and the décor was nothing special, painted in stone neutrals. It had wooden floors but the ceilings were high and the windows flooded the place with light.

'What do you think?' asked Mum as we walked though.

I gave her a hug by way of reply. We'd stayed in some of the finest hotels in the world, had our spacious lovely home in Richmond, but this small flat, with its box bedroom for me, felt like the height of luxury. I loved it.

'And do you think we could maybe get our bed linen out of storage?' I asked.

'Most definitely,' said Dad. 'I don't think I could sleep another night on those lumpy pillows.'

Mum laughed. 'I think we could bring a few things here, don't you?' she asked.

'Definitely,' he replied. He went over to the windows in the sitting room and looked out. 'And this won't be forever . . . but it will do for now. It will definitely do.'

I went and stood by him and put my arm around his waist.

'And your dad has a business idea, don't you, Patrick?' said Mum.

Dad nodded. 'Don't want to say too much about it yet, Louise. Don't want to jinx it. Early days. Early days.'

'I'm sure it will be brilliant whatever it is,' I said.

Dad grinned. 'Actually I think it is. Watch this space, kiddo. Mr Lord has arrived in town.'

I hadn't seen either of them so happy in ages.

After our viewing, I set off for town to meet the girls. The sunshine had brought out the tourists and the streets were full of people enjoying the weather. Even though I'd only been in Bath a short while, I was getting familiar with the city and easily found my way up to our meeting point.

Tasmin and Clover were already there, standing outside the deli with a group of boys, some of whom I recognised from school. Aiden, Ed, Chas (Clover's boyfriend) and Stu (Tasmin's ex). They were all friendly, said hi, and I noticed Luke checking me out but he wasn't my type, nor were any of the rest of them. There was only one boy for me and he was Alex Taylor. Since Allegra had told me that he was coming to Bath, I couldn't stop thinking about him.

As we stood chatting for a while, I could hear music coming from the car park, which was halfway down a slope opposite where there were a crowd of people standing in front of a stage to the left. Others were at various stalls lining the pavement in front of the slope and the smell of frying onions, bacon and burgers filled the air.

We set off to join the crowds in the car park and I filled Tasmin and Clover in on the new flat.

'We're moving in a couple of weeks,' I said.

'Yay,' said Tasmin. 'I'll get my room back.'

'Don't mind her,' said Clover and she squeezed my arm.

'I don't. It means I get my own space again too. So double yay.'

'Invite us over,' said Clover.

'We'll have a sleepover. Housewarming sort of thing,' Tasmin added.

I laughed. We were just about to get our space back and she wanted to come and share again but I took it as a compliment. She wanted to stay friends.

As soon as we had our place by a wall towards the back, Tasmin started surveying the crowd. Over to the left, halfway into the crowd, I noticed Niall. He was surrounded by girls and had his arm around one of them. He glanced over at our group and when he saw me, he waved and then put his index finger up for a moment as though asking me to wait a second. He leant over to get something out of the carrier bag at his feet. It looked like it was full of groceries. He pulled something out, held it and pointed at it and then at himself. He was holding up a jar of Marmite. First he looked at the jar with a big smile and then changed his expression to one of disgust, like bleurgh. I got it. Marmite, you either love it or hate it.

I laughed, then I pulled the bleurgh face back at him and he nodded and laughed too. *What a cheek*, I thought, flirting with me when he was with someone else. The girl he was with looked at him quizzically and he put the jar back in the carrier bag then appeared to be explaining the joke to her. The girl glanced over at me then turned her back. I turned away too and scanned the rest of the crowd.

'Looking for someone?' asked Stu.

'Sort of,' I replied.

'A mystery boy,' said Tasmin. 'He made a CD and Paige wants to know who he is.'

'CD? How very quaint. Have you got it with you?' Stu asked.

I shook my head. 'It's at home but whoever made it has to be local because all of the tracks are local bands.'

'And we know that one of the bands is playing today. Black Pearl,' added Clover. 'They're on in an hour.'

I made a mental note to always carry the CD with me as we listened to the band on stage and I continued scanning the audience. After about ten minutes, the band playing left and a boy of about nineteen got up to play his guitar. As soon as he started singing, I recognised his voice. He was the singer of the ballad that was track one on the CD.

'Do you know who he is?' I whispered to Stu.

'Callum Casey,' said Stu. 'Used to go to our school.'

I went back to listening and moved forward in order to hear better. He wasn't singing the same song as the CD but another song that was similar. I liked the look of him too. He wasn't exactly stand-out good-looking, but he had something. He was tall with shoulder-length hair and the indie look that most of the musicians in Bath had. I pushed further into the crowd. For a split second, Callum looked straight at me. I felt a bolt of electricity. *Maybe Callum is Mystery Boy*, I thought as his glance moved away from me and across the rest of the audience. Maybe Mystery Boy's a musician? That would make sense and be why his track was number one and why he chose local bands for his CD. They could all be his mates.

Callum did a couple of numbers then got up to leave. I watched him go backstage, down some steps to the right then disappear. Another band came on and the lead singer went straight to the main microphone.

'We need a drummer,' he said. 'Anyone out there who can drum? Our guy's just been dragged off by his parents. He wasn't supposed to be here.' The crowd laughed but no one got up to drum. The band did a set but I didn't like their music so I went back to join the others at the back. Not long after, Painted Asparagus came on. They were from the CD too. I recognised their name and their sound. They were good, really good, with great vocals. To the right of the stage, I noticed that Callum Casey had reappeared and was watching the band playing from the side of the car park.

'Do you think he's here then?' asked Tasmin.

'Mystery Boy?' I replied. 'I bet he is.' I looked over at Callum again. 'But how would we know for sure without going up to loads of boys and asking them . . .' An idea suddenly struck me. 'Unless we ask someone to put out an announcement from the stage. What do you think?'

Tasmin shrugged. 'What would we say?'

'Er . . . something like, "Can the boy who made a home-made CD recently please come to the stage?" No, it's a mad idea.'

'No it's not,' said Tasmin. 'I'm going to go and ask them to do it.' She jumped down from the wall and raced forward before I could stop her. Moments later, I saw her talking to a man to the right of the stage. When Painted Asparagus had finished their set, the man got up and went centre stage. 'A big hand for Painted Asparagus. Thanks guys. Next to play will be

White Light. And a short announcement, or request. Can a boy who recently made a home-made CD come to the right of the stage? Someone is looking for you.'

She should have mentioned the title of the CD, I thought as Clover quickly extracted herself from Chas's arms. 'Ohmygod,' she said and she grabbed my hand and pulled me in the direction of the stage. As we passed the area where Niall had been, I noticed that he'd moved and gone back up towards the road and was standing in the queue at a hot-dog stall chatting to yet another girl.

The man who'd made the announcement was waiting with Tasmin. We weren't the only ones heading their way. About ten boys were gathering around him.

'What's this about?' asked a chubby dark-haired boy with a sweet face. 'Are you collecting demos? Our band has a demo.'

The man winked at Tasmin. 'Over to you kiddo,' he said.

The boys turned en masse to look at her. I quickly scanned the group, who were all looking eagerly at Tasmin.

'We're not collecting demos,' she explained. 'We're looking for a boy who recently made a home-made CD.'

'What do you mean?' asked the chubby boy.

'CD. Home-made. You know, a compilation of favourite tracks sort of thing,' Tasmin explained.

'Well we all probably did at some point,' said a tall blond boy. 'We're all musicians. What's this about?'

'So you're not a talent scout?' another blond boy asked.

'No,' said Tasmin and there was a groan of disappointment.

'We're looking for the boy who made a CD of local bands called *Songs for Sarah*.' I added.

'Why?' the chubby boy asked Tasmin.

'My friend's looking for him,' she replied. She looked my way and the group turned to me. Of course, I went bright red.

'What's this CD got on it? You need to be more specific,' said chubby boy.

'It starts with Callum Casey,' I said. 'It's got Painted Asparagus on it and Black Pearl.'

'Not me,' said one of the boys and turned away, as did a few others.

'Did you say *Songs for Sarah*?' asked the chubby boy. 'Where did you get it?'

'In a charity shop,' I replied.

'Charity shop? So why do you want to know who made it?' he asked.

'She liked it,' said Tasmin.

'Is that all?' he asked.

'What do you mean is that all?' said Clover. 'I think that's as good a reason as any.'

I felt excruciatingly embarrassed. Everyone was looking at me.

Suddenly a voice from the back of the crowd spoke up and everyone turned to look. It was Callum Casey. 'I think it's romantic.' He smiled at me and I noticed that he had kind eyes. 'So, can you tell us a bit more about it.'

'Well . . .' I started. 'It's got a face on the front. A girl's face, torn up and placed over a photo.'

'Not me,' said another boy in the group and the rest of them began to disperse. I heard one of them grumbling something about Tasmin being a tease.

'I thought it was someone from a recording company,' said one as he walked off. 'It's just some kid on a wild goose chase.'

'Sorry,' I called after them.

'No, it was a good idea,' said Tasmin. I wasn't so sure. I felt embarrassed by the whole scene.

I noticed that Callum and the chubby boy hadn't left with the others. 'So you liked this CD?' asked Callum.

I nodded. 'Yes. I . . . I just wondered who'd made it, that's all.'

'Was it you?' asked Tasmin.

Callum shook his head. 'Nah. I've made CDs. Course I have. Who doesn't put together their own collections? But I do it all on computer or straight onto my MP3 player.'

'I liked your set,' I said to him.

He smiled again. 'Thanks.'

'I'm going back to join Chaz,' said Clover and headed off back into the crowd as the next band began to play.

'Me too,' said Tasmin. She glanced at me then Callum. 'Coming, Paige?'

'Unless you fancy a coffee,' said the chubby boy.

'Yeah, you go,' said Tasmin, making up my mind for me. 'Text me. Laters.' And she was gone after Clover.

'I . . . Oh. OK,' I said. Maybe he could tell me a bit more about the music scene and give me another clue. At the same time, I felt disappointed that it wasn't Callum who hadn't asked me for coffee. He was hanging about too. 'Want to join us?' I asked him.

He shook his head. 'Love to but I've got to meet a mate,' he said and turned to leave. 'See you around maybe.'

'So you're stuck with me,' said the chubby boy. 'I'm Sean but my friends called me FB.'

'FB. For Facebook?'

'No. FB for fat boy.'

I was shocked. 'You're not fat,' I said.

He grinned. 'I'm not thin either,' he said. 'A mate used to call me fat boy then it got shortened to FB and it stuck.'

'I'm Paige,' I said.

'You're new to Bath, aren't you? I noticed you in town one day with Tasmin.'

'Oh, did you?' I asked, then hoped that he wasn't hurt that I hadn't noticed him. 'I'm . . . er . . . still finding my way around, getting to know people.'

'Sure,' he said. 'Takes time.'

'So you know Tasmin?'

'By sight,' he said. 'Small town.' He pointed at one of the stalls selling coffee and indicated we should head over there.

We got coffees then sat on a wall, got chatting and he told me that he was in the upper sixth at a school on the other side of Bath and doing similar subjects to me.

'How you getting on?' he asked after I'd filled him in a little on why I had moved to Bath. 'Must be hard having changed halfway through Year Ten. Bet you miss your mates.'

'I'm getting used to it. I like my art teacher, Mr Jolliffe,' I said. 'He's really enthusiastic and encouraging.'

FB nodded. 'Yeah, I know him. He's cool. He's a musician too.'

I laughed. 'Seems that half of Bath are either musicians or artists. My uncle's a musician too. He works at my school. Mr Davidson.'

'Oh, right. Yeah I know him too. He's OK. And yeah, there are loads of musicians. Me too. There must something in the water here. Mr Jolliffe organises the festivals in the park by the Crescent every year. I'm going to help him with the next one. It's called Zoom and is a battle of the bands sort of thing. All the local bands play. The next one is in early summer. We thought we'd have a theme. Make it more interesting, like the Venice carnival, so we were going to ask everyone to wear a mask.'

'No way!' I said. 'I've been to the Venice carnival and I'm doing a project on masks. I was doing portraits but it's evolved.'

'Really. I did a mask project last year. Sadly the mask idea for the festival got voted out. Shame. I think that everyone in masks could have been interesting.'

'Me too.'

After that we were off, talking like long-lost friends. He was also interested in the CD and what it meant to me. After I'd I filled him in on all the details, he smiled. 'I can see it means a lot to you to find whoever made it,' he said.

'I guess it does. I'm not sure why.'

'Go with your gut,' he said. 'Sometimes things defy explanation – and who knows where it will lead? Like already, we've met up because of the CD.'

'What's your band called?'

'Undercurrent.'

'Yes, I think I remember that name. Your track is somewhere towards the end. A sad song.'

'That's me,' said FB and pulled a comical sad face.

I liked him. He was easy to get on with and unlike some boys, he listened as much as he talked. By the end of the afternoon, we'd swapped phone numbers and email addresses and promised to meet up again. Although I had no more clues about Mystery Boy, I'd found a new friend.

Chapter Fifteen

FB was true to his word and didn't waste any time getting in touch with me. He texted me the following week and suggested that I go over to his house on Wednesday evening after school.

'Why does he want to meet at his house?' asked Tasmin when we met up at lunchtime in the common room. 'It's a bit fast, isn't it?'

'So we can play *Songs for Sarah*,' I replied as I spooned coffee granules into two mugs. 'He said he'd see what he could do to help me find whoever had made it.

'I'll go with you,' said Tasmin. 'In case he tries something.'

'We're just friends.'

'Yeah right.'

'I'll be fine. I trust him,' I said.

Tasmin rolled her eyes. 'Much as I've come to like you, dear Paige, I am going to tell you a home truth and that is that you're naive, especially when it comes to boys.'

I laughed. She really does speak her mind. 'How do you know?'

She tapped the side of her nose. 'I just know.'

'I'm not that naive. I think I know FB's type. He's a sweetie. I'll be fine really.'

'I'll be the judge of that so I'll be going with you,' she said. I didn't mind. It felt nice that she was looking out for me. 'Do you fancy him?'

'No,' I said. 'It's not like that. We get on, that's all.'

'Hmm. Not sure he'll see it that way,' said Tasmin. 'So tell me, Paige, how many boys have you kissed?'

'I . . . er . . .' I felt myself blush. 'Only one and that wasn't a boy I liked.'

'I thought so,' said Tasmin.

'To be truthful, I do worry that I won't be any good at it.'

Tasmin smiled. 'Don't worry. When it's the right boy, you will. It will come naturally. I'm sure you'll be good at it, but boys . . . well, that's another matter.'

'What do you mean?'

'There are boys that come on too strong and stick their tongue in your mouth and it's all too wet and full on.'

'Yuk.'

'And those that don't know what to do at all, and give you a dry, closed-mouthed kiss. That's not nice either.'

'Where are they or me supposed to learn? They don't teach it in schools. I mean, there's so much I don't know.'

'Ask away,' said Tasmin. 'You're talking to the expert.'

I had to laugh. She was completely serious and luckily the common room was empty apart from the two of us. Everyone else was outside soaking up the sun. 'OK. Do you keep your eyes closed or open? Do you keep your mouth open and if so, how much? And your tongue? Does it go in-out or in and around?'

This time, it was Tasmin's turn to laugh but I didn't feel she was being unkind. I wanted to know, and who better than someone like her who had had boyfriends? My questions certainly weren't the kind I could ask my mum.

'You really haven't had much experience, have you?' said Tasmin.

'No, I haven't,' I admitted.

'First of all, don't stress it,' said Tasmin. 'With the right boy, it will all come naturally and you'll find you know exactly what to do. It will feel nice – great, in fact, if it's right. I'd say eyes closed when you're kissing. No boy wants to open his eyes to find he's eyeball to eyeball with you. After a bit of kissing, you can introduce the tongue, but when it feels right. Keep it light to begin with – tender, gentle – then if it feels good, you can get more passionate and, believe me, your tongue will know what to do. And sometimes boys like a bit of lip nibbling. That can feel really good. But not too much – it's not like he's your supper.'

'God, I'll never get it right. It sounds like a science. Gentle, tender. Trust your tongue. Bit of nibbling. Eyes shut. But what if I miss his mouth?'

'You keep them open until your lips touch, then close them.'

'Right,' I said, but I can't say I felt any more confident after her tuition.

'Anyway, enough about snogging. Have you had any more ideas about finding your mystery boy?'

'Actually I have been thinking about it. Instead of trying to find him, how about I try to find Sarah? The girl that Mystery Boy made the CD for? She might be local. She may even go to our school. If I can find her, I could ask her who made the CD for her. She tells me. Simple.'

Tasmin nodded. 'Not a bad idea. So what do you suggest?'

'I could put a notice in the library as a start. I could put a postcard up today saying if you're the Sarah some boy made a CD for, please contact Paige Lord or Tasmin Davidson in Year Ten.

'Better she contacts me than you as a lot of people still won't know who you are,' said Tasmin. 'Just put my name and maybe Clover's. Everyone knows who she is too.'

'Good point. And if that doesn't work, I could go to the school office and ask the secretary for a list of all the pupils here. She could be in any year.'

'OK, and if she's not at this school, what then?' asked Tasmin.

'I will rethink the plan. As you keep telling me, Bath's a small place.'

When it got to Wednesday, FB came to meet me at the school gates. He didn't seem so happy about Tasmin coming along and was quiet when we caught the bus to his house. His silence didn't last long and as soon as we got to his terraced house, he took us up to his room and pulled out all the books he had on masks. His room was a bit like Tasmin's in that every surface was cluttered, in his case with books, magazines, DVDs, computer games and CDs. The walls were plastered with posters of various bands, one of The Smiths in prime position, and one wall was covered ceiling to floor with amazing masks. I was about to ask if he'd made them when he thrust a book into my hand.

'Take a look at that while I find something,' he said.

I sat on his bed and started to look through the book he'd given me. It had great examples of African masks, many I hadn't seen before. Tasmin sat next to me and did her best to look interested but I could tell immediately that it wasn't her thing. FB went over to his computer. 'I've been dying to show you all these since I met you, Paige,' he said as he punched a few keys to open a file. 'I've got loads of images on here.'

'I don't think we want to see the images you have hidden on your computer,' said Tasmin. 'Not if they're like the ones most teenage boys look at.' She laughed. FB didn't.

Tasmin lasted about fifteen minutes. I could tell by her left foot that she was bored out her mind because as FB and I looked through the pages of masks, her foot started twitching, up and down, up and down as if she was already walking out of there.

She soon was.

'I'll see you at home later, hey? Text me when you're on your way,' she said as she got up and made for the door.

I had to laugh. When did you turn into my mother? I wanted to ask but I bit back the words.

FB and I spent an hour or so pouring over all his findings about masks. He did have some great images and looking at them gave me lots of ideas for my project. He was also generous about lending me some stuff to take home to study further.

I pointed at the masks on the wall. 'Did you make those?'

He nodded. 'Most of them.'

I pointed to two simple masks that were next to each other – a white one showing a happy face and a black one with an exaggerated sad face. 'I like the Shakespearian ones,' I said.

FB nodded. 'Ah. The only two I didn't make. Those were made by a mate. He gave them to me when he realised that I'd been making and collecting them. The whole thing about masks resonates with me. I'm interested in the psychology too. We wear masks for different people, to hide our thoughts and feelings, a protection of sorts, don't you think?'

'I do,' I replied. 'That's the angle I want to take in my project. I'm not going to make actual masks. I want to draw and paint the more subtle masks that people wear. Like that saying, put on a brave face. I'll do a series of brave faces . . .'

'Cheery faces, happy faces, flirty faces. My mum always used to say, "Put on your happy face",' FB added.

'My mum's been doing that lately with all the changes that have been happening in my life. Her and Dad.' I'd told him a bit about the move from London when we were chatting at the festival.

'What about you?' FB asked. He had a gentle expression in his eyes and looked at me as though genuinely interested in what was going on inside me. For a moment, I thought I was going to cry but didn't feel that I knew FB well enough to let him know what I'd been going through. *And things are getting better*, I told myself.

'I'm OK,' I said.

He sat next to me on the bed, put his arm around me and gave me a squeeze. 'And there's your brave-face mask, right there,' he said.

I wasn't sure how I felt about him having his arm around me but he didn't keep it there for long. He got up and went to the door. 'Fancy a drink? Tea? Coffee? Juice?'

'Juice, thanks,' I replied. While he was away, I flicked through a file he'd pulled out with the others. Masks in Shakespeare. The pages were full of quotes and sketches of masks used in various plays.

FB came back with a tray with glasses, a carton of apple juice and plate of biscuits. 'Help yourself,' he said as he put it down on the cabinet next to his bed. I was about to ask him about the notes in his file when he asked, 'How about we listen to this CD of yours?'

I got it out of my bag and he put it into his computer then we both lay back. He gave me the bed and he lay on the floor, his head resting on a beanbag. Callum Casey's voice filled the air. FB only spoke to say, 'My band,' when his track played.

When the last track had finished, FB sat up. 'So you like this CD, do you?'

'I do. I really do.'

'It's a good compilation. It tells a story, doesn't it? A love story – guy sees girl, falls in love but did she feel the same? Or was it about a fantasy girl.'

'I know. I wonder what happened.'

He glanced at the cover and I told him all that I'd worked out about how it was put together. Like Tasmin and I had done, he reached for a magnifying glass to see if he could find any more clues. 'Tell you what, I'll scan the cover in on the scanner at school,' said FB. 'Then we can blow it up and see if there are any more clues on there. Apart from that, all I can help with are the bands. I know all of them. All local. Yeah, whoever put this CD together has good taste in music especially as my band is on there.'

Excellent, we're making progress, I thought as I drank my juice.

Chapter Sixteen

Mystery Boy

"The sight of lovers feedeth those in love."
Shakespeare: As You Like It – Act 3, scene 4.

The deed is done. She has the CD and I know her name. Sarah. It happened by accident. Maybe fate? I was in Costa Coffee down in town and she came in. My first instinct was to turn away but didn't because she doesn't know me yet. I watched as she joined friends. A bunch of girls from Kingswood school who'd been checking me out before she came in. 'Hey Sarah,' I heard one of them say.

Sarah was a pickpocket's dream because she left her bag behind the chair she took. It was gaping open. I'd be able to drop the CD in there no problem. I got up to go to the loos – once in there, I pulled out the envelope with the CD in it and wrote 'Songs for Sarah' on the envelope and the spine of the CD cover. *Perfect*, I thought. It made it all the more personal. When I came out, I saw she'd gone with the girls to the counter and her bag was still there on the floor. Cupid was smiling on me. I dropped the envelope into her bag. Easy peasy. Job done.

Chapter Seventeen

Best day of my life, I texted Allegra on the Friday of the bank holiday. *New home, new chapter.*

Can't w8 to see you tmro. Call me l8r. I have nws of Alex, she texted back.

Of course, on reading the part about Alex, I couldn't wait and called her straight away, but she must have just switched her phone off after she'd texted me because it went to messages. It was bank holiday weekend and she was coming down on the train for the day with her mum. The plan was that her mum was going to head for the spa and I was going to show Allegra round. I couldn't wait.

'You got everything you need?' asked Mum.

'Yep,' I called back. We were in the new flat.

Mum and Dad had moved in during the day and after school, instead of heading back to Aunt Karen's, I'd made my way to our new home where I'd spent a glorious evening arranging my bedroom. I'd packed my bags last night and Mum and Dad had brought them over first thing in the morning so that they were there when I arrived. Removal vans had been in the morning too and when I got there, it gave me a warm glow to see familiar items from our old home in Richmond piled up in the sitting room ready to find their place. I soon got busy helping Mum empty the boxes, filling kitchen cupboards, making beds (lovely, lovely soft cotton) and putting clothes away.

'It's weird,' I said to Mum as we unrolled a blue and taupe Persian rug out in the sitting room, 'it's like we've been in a parallel universe for a month but now we've come back to reality.'

Mum nodded. 'I guess,' she pointed at the rug, 'we've landed alright but somewhere different.'

'It's going to be OK though, isn't it?'

'I hope so.'

'How's Dad's business idea coming along?' I asked.

Mum glanced at the door to check if Dad was nearby. 'Slowly,' she said. 'I'm not supposed to say anything but . . . he's found some premises that are coming up for rent. A shop to be precise. He's been researching where there might be a gap in the market here in Bath but that's the problem. Everything's just about covered – cafés, shops selling merchandise, knick-knacks. It has to be the right product.'

'He'll think of something,' I said. 'How's he going to finance it?'

Mum rolled her eyes. 'Loan of course.'

'I thought he couldn't get a loan any more.'

'He can't but your Aunt Karen and Uncle Mike can. They've agreed to be investors if they like his ideas.'

'Wow. That's good of them.'

'I know but they also stand to make some money if things work out, which will be good for them as they both only have small pensions. They believe in your dad. None of what happened was his fault and he still has a brilliant business head on him, if only we can think of the right product. There are a million tour-ists piling off buses here every day, even in the winter. There has to be something we can provide.'

'Ice cream?' I suggested. 'No, bad idea, there are loads of ice cream places near the centre. Loads of fudge shops too.'

'We'll think of something. It's not something for you to worry about.'

Too late, my mind was already whirring with mad ideas as I went back to my room. Masks? T-shirts? I wanted to help.

Dad had arranged for my old dressing table and mirror to be brought out of storage, a desk that used to be in a downstairs study, a bedside cabinet and a bed that used to be in one of our spare rooms in the Richmond house. My old bed was much too big for the new room but I didn't care. Anything would be more comfortable than the camp bed I'd been sleeping on. By bedtime, I had made the room my own. My wine-coloured bedspread and cushions were on the bed, curtains up across the window (they were a bit long but Mum said she could shorten them easily), a Turkish rug on the floor, my clothes folded and put away in drawers or hanging in the built-in wardrobe in the corner and there was a bedside lamp casting a soft light into the room. It looked fab.

I put my laptop on the desk, lit the scented candle that Mum had bought me as a house-warming present, arranged a few books and files, then lay back on my bed for a few minutes. I felt like I could breathe again and stayed there for a while, savouring the moment.

Order had been restored in my life, I felt a wave of happiness surge through me.

My phone beeped that I had a text. It was FB asking how the move had gone. I texted back: *happy, feel like I'm at home again*. He was proving to be a good friend and we'd met up a few times to hang out, have a coffee or talk about what we were into. I liked the fact he was so into art and we could talk about that – something I could never do with Tasmin.

When I got up to get a drink before going to sleep, Mum and Dad were still arranging and rearranging furniture in the sitting room.

'I love it here,' I said.

Dad laughed. 'It's an eighth of the size of our old house and has no garden but I know what you mean. I love it too.'

Tasmin and Clover came over the next morning to have the flat tour and both gave it the thumbs-up. They'd brought house-warming presents too: a bunch of flowers from Clover and a couple of mags from Tasmin.

'She's read them both,' said Clover as she flopped on my bed.

'It's the thought,' said Tasmin as she opened my wardrobe and had a nosey inside. 'Tidy huh? So, new house. I can't tell you how fab it is to have my room back as well.'

'I can imagine,' I said.

'And we have some news for you,' said Tasmin. 'Well not exactly news but I managed to persuade Jess Bendall to ask her mum, who's school secretary, to let me have a list of all the names of girls at our school.' She pulled out a sheaf of A4 paper and gave it to me.

'We trawled through it last night,' Clover added. 'You wouldn't believe how many Sarahs there are at our school. Forty.'

'Do you think we should contact them all?' I asked.

'Yep. We found a few on our school's Facebook page and we've sent them messages. Eight have replied. Not them, so they're off this list.'

'Wow, thanks,' I said. I was really touched that they'd spent so much time looking for me.

'We're a team,' said Tasmin. 'And you're not the only one with detective skills.'

'And if Sarah's not at our school, we can start on the others in the area,' said Clover. 'There are loads of schools in Bath.'

'That's if she lives in Bath,' I said. 'What if she's from Bristol?'

Tasmin gave me a stern look. 'We have to start somewhere,' she said.

'Hey, why don't we start a detective agency when we leave school?' I said. 'With our combined skills, we'd be brilliant.'

'Nah. I want to go on my gap year,' said Tasmin.

'And I want to open my vintage shop,' said Clover. 'Or do something in fashion.'

'Talking of which, we were thinking on the way over that we should do a makeover on you,' Tasmin continued as she pulled out a few of my clothes. 'Get you wearing some colour.'

'*You* were thinking,' said Clover. 'I think she's fine as she is.'

Tasmin rolled her eyes. 'You're joking. I mean look at this stuff in here – navy, cream, white, navy, navy, navy, boring. You dress like a nun, Paige.'

'Thanks, Tasmin. I'm glad you approve. But makeover? To what?'

Tasmin looked me up and down. 'Not sure yet. You could be really good-looking if you tried.'

Clover burst out laughing. 'You have some cheek, Tas.'

I laughed too. I was getting used to Tasmin's outspokenness and decided to give her some of her own medicine. I looked at her in exactly the same way she'd been looking at me. Up and down. Critically. Her orange face. Make-up. The hair extensions.

'What? *What?*' she asked.

'OK. A makeover. If I let you do a makeover on me, you have to let me do one on you.'

Tasmin looked shocked.

'Touché, Tas,' said Clover. 'You've met your match.'

'Yes but *I* don't need a makeover.'

I gave her a look as if to say, 'Yeah right'. 'OK, but you could be a very attractive girl if you wanted.'

Clover cracked up. 'Now then girls,' she said.

'So what do I need to change?' asked Tasmin. 'Seriously, come on.'

For a moment, I hesitated. I didn't want to upset her but then I knew she wouldn't hold back when it was my turn. 'OK. Mainly I'd tone it down. The make-up for a start. You wear too much and you really don't need to. I've seen you first thing in the morning and know that you've got a very pretty face.'

'Don't try and sugar it. What else?' Tasmin demanded.

'Your hair looks scruffy with those extensions. I'd like to see it with a gloss on it. Get rid of them.'

Clover gasped. 'Go girl. And . . . actually I agree.'

Tasmin turned to her. 'You're supposed to be my friend!'

'I am,' Clover replied, 'but if you're going to dish it, you got to eat it too.'

Tasmin made a rude gesture with her fingers by way of reply.

'And I'd put you in something prettier too,' I continued. 'Not girlie but . . . mm, I'm not sure about the dress style I'd pick for you, but I'd definitely get rid of the heels you wear outside school. You struggle in them, they're throwing your back out and you don't walk in an attractive way because of it.'

When I saw that Tasmin's jaw was on her chest, I thought I'd better stop. The part of me that was growing more confident seemed to be coming more to the fore lately but I didn't want to lose friends over it. I was going to mention the fake eyelashes, but all in good time. I glanced at Clover who had suddenly decided that there was something really interesting out the window and started humming in a casual way, though I could see she was really having a hard time not cracking up laughing again.

'OK,' said Tasmin. 'The gauntlet has been thrown. You make me over. I don't have to dress your way forever but I'm open to new ideas. I'll show you I am.

And in the same way, you have to let me dress you for a day.'

Clover looked back into the room. 'I've had a great idea. Frome. Let's go to Frome.'

'What's Frome? A dress shop?'

Clover shook her head. 'It's a town not far from here.'

'We can get the train,' said Tasmin and looked in her purse. 'I've got enough.'

'Me too,' said Clover.

'How much do I need?' I asked.

'About a fiver,' said Tasmin. 'Brilliant idea, Clover.'

'So what's in Frome?' I asked.

But Clover and Tasmin were already on their feet ready to go. 'You'll find out,' said Clover.

Chapter Eighteen

After I'd let Mum and Dad know where I was going, Tasmin, Clover and I caught the train from Bath Spa. Tasmin and Clover sat on the right of the compartment and I took a seat on the left by the window. As they texted mates and chatted away, I listened to my iPod and gazed out of the window. Woodlands, canals, pretty villages flashed by, then a town called Bradford-on-Avon which looked like a mini Bath with rows and rows of old houses going up the hills.

'What you listening to?' asked Clover from over the aisle.

I shrugged. 'It's on random,' I replied. Actually I was listening to *Songs for Sarah* again. I was so familiar with it now that I knew almost all the tracks word for word. I didn't want to admit to Clover or Tasmin how many times I'd listened to it in case they thought I was getting obsessive. But I *was* obsessed with it. I couldn't help myself. Every time I heard the lyrics in the songs, I felt that they had been chosen for me. I wondered for the hundredth time where was the boy who had made it? Even though I knew that Alex would soon be down in Bath, I couldn't help but doubt that he would ever really fancy me or that anything could happen between us.

Mystery Boy was my fantasy and in my imagination, he was perfect, we were made for each other and I didn't have to worry if I said the wrong thing or didn't look cool enough because it was all in my head, a daydream where I controlled what happened. It gave me a buzz to think that he was alive somewhere and that he had a life, friends, a family, a bedroom. What was he doing at this moment? Having a lie-in? Or out with mates somewhere enjoying the sun? Or maybe, like me, travelling on a train gazing out of a window? Or maybe he was with Sarah? Or had she dumped him or not been interested? That made sense or else why would the CD have ended up in a charity shop? If I'd been given the CD, I would have treasured it and never given it away.

I opened one eye to see what Clover and Tasmin were doing. They were still busy chatting so I went back to my thoughts. It made me feel good to think of the boy as real with a life somewhere as well as in my dreams. So, I asked myself, *had he been disappointed or rejected by Sarah?* Whatever had happened, he was somewhere living, breathing and possibly, not a million miles from Bath. I was sure we'd meet one day. I started to daydream how that would be. Would it be at a gig? In a coffee shop? At school? Would we recognise that we were soul mates?

The words of the Black Pearl track played in my headphones:

> I want a love that's sharp as a diamond
> And as warm as a fireside chair,
> A love that's for now and forever.
> And when I find it I'm sure you'll be there.

I felt certain that when I met Mystery Boy we'd understand each other and what each other wanted perfectly. As more trees, a river and open fields flashed by, an upbeat track by a female artist called Lady B began and I began to think about my future.

The song was about making your memories and not letting life slip into being ordinary or mundane.

I'd be an artist. I'd dress in the most fabulous clothes. I'd have my own style. I'd have my flat in London with Allegra – original artworks everywhere, Venetian masks on the wall and on the shelves would be my books and a few old favourite CDs. *Songs for Sarah* would be there in the same way that Mum and Dad keep a box of CDs from when they were younger, tracks that they treasure because they make them feel nostalgic about a past time or place. *Songs for Sarah* would forever evoke the spring and summer of this year, the time when my life changed and I moved to Bath. There would be more to the memories of this time than just the move. Memories yet to be made. Memories of when I meet the boy behind the CD. The boy in shadow on the back cover. The boy who could talk to my heart through music. All I had to do was find him.

Tasmin nudged my leg. 'Hey, sleepy head. We're almost there. You've been miles away. What have you been dreaming about?'

'I was thinking about . . . thinking about my future but also about my past. I was in my future looking at things from the past. Things that are happening now. I was thinking about memories that I've yet to make.'

Tasmin looked at me as though I was mad. I've noticed that she does that a lot. 'Right . . . That's clear then. Not.'

'Awesome,' said Clover as the train drew into Frome station and we got up to wait for the doors to open. 'Memories you've yet to make. Love it. It's romantic.'

'It's daft,' said Tasmin.

Once out of the cool shadows inside the station, it was a bright sunny day and our moods matched the weather as we walked into town. When we got there, I looked around but couldn't make out what was so special and why we hadn't spent the day in Bath, which is a shopaholic's dream. All I could see were a couple of charity shops, a shop selling cheap shoes and a pub.

'Over here,' said Clover and she started to lead us up a steep cobbled hill lined with shops. 'The best vintage shops in the south-west.' She pulled me into the shop in front of us. Inside, it was full of old clothes jammed onto rails and piled up on shelves. *I can see why Tasmin would like this place*, I thought, *it looks exactly like her bedroom.*

For the next hour, we had a brilliant time. We tried on hats from the 1940s, dresses from the 1950s and 60s, big old fur coats, bits of lace, earrings, fans, shoes. Clover made me try on a top hat and a black Victorian jacket with a tiny waist. 'Very Goth, darling,' she said when I came out of the changing room. The jacket was a bit small but, I had to admit, it looked cool especially when Clover teamed it with a flared red-and-black flowered skirt from the Fifties. I'd never have thought of putting them together, but they worked and made me look interesting and daring, not safe and sensible. I loved the change.

'So what's the difference between vintage and second hand?' I asked as we sifted through baskets of beautiful silk scarves.

'Hmm, good question,' said Clover who was trying on a fabulous velvet cloak. 'Vintage is older and more expensive. And vintage is way more stylish than the stuff in most charity shops, though you can find bargains in them too, but look at the detail, the sewing skill, in some of these clothes. Fabulous. And don't forget, some of the Hollywood celebs wear vintage on Oscar night now and they're often the loveliest dresses.'

I had to admit she was right. Some of the dresses in the shop had trims and finishes that were beautiful.

'This shop reminds me of those places where you can go to have your photo taken in old clothes,' I said. 'There's one in Eton. Mum and I dressed up as Victorian ladies and Dad dressed up as gentleman complete with top hat and curly moustache when we were there once. It was a great memento of the day.'

'Yeah, photograph,' said Tasmin and she whipped out her phone and took a shot of Clover in the cloak. After that, there was no stopping us, and as we went further up the hill, from shop to shop, we took photos of each of us dressed in all sorts of weird and wonderful outfits. As I looked at myself in the various mirrors in different colours and fabrics, I could see the old Paige disappearing and another girl starting to emerge.

After an hour, I spotted a knee-length coral cotton dress with tiny cornflower-blue flowers on it. It looked like a Forties dress and vintage is usually Clover's thing, but this one had Tasmin's name on it. 'Perfect,' I said. 'Tasmin, try this on.'

Her expression was priceless. 'Ew.'

'Come on, Tas,' said Clover and she took the dress and held it up against her. 'Play the game.'

Tasmin disappeared into the changing room and emerged five minutes later with the dress on. It fitted her perfectly and she looked fabulous. She looked in the mirror and did a twirl.

'Hey, you look like a girl,' said Clover.

'Meaning?' asked Tasmin. 'What did I look like before? A gorilla?'

'I mean it suits you,' said Clover. 'How much is it?'

Tasmin looked at the label. 'Fifteen pounds. I don't have it.'

'I do,' said Clover. 'I'm going to get it for your birthday – early present – and you have to wear it.'

Tasmin was studying herself in the mirror. I could see that she was pleased with what she saw. 'Well, OK,' she said. 'I guess I could wear it around the house when there's no one to see, or it might look OK with a pair of cowboy boots or red heels and red scarf in my hair, like you wear, Clover.'

'That would look great,' I said.

When she went back into the changing room, Clover high-fived me. 'Good choice. She'd have never picked out anything like that. It's good to go shopping with someone with a fresh eye. You next,' she said and started searching the rails.

She picked out two dresses and two tops for me to try. One dress was strong blue, the other fuchsia, and both tops were red. She held them up against me.

'Jewel colours would look good on you with your dark eyes and hair. You play it far too safe in the colours and styles you pick.'

I took the clothes and went to try them on. None of them fitted properly but Clover was right. The stronger colours did look good on me. Tasmin stuck her head around the changing room curtain then pulled it back. 'Wow. Much better. Those colours make you look . . . I don't know . . . Spanish or Italian. Exotic, that's for sure.' She got out her make-up and applied a little red gloss to my lips then stood back to look. 'Fab. Don't you think, Clover?'

Clover came to join us. 'Deffo.' She looked at our reflections in the mirror. 'It's like you need a bit of Tas, Paige, and she needs a bit of you.'

Tasmin laughed. 'You can blunt my pencil a bit and I'll sharpen yours.'

'OK, later when we're back from Frome, I'll do your make-up. You do mine,' I said.

'Deal,' said Tasmin.

Clover went and paid for the dress for Tasmin, then we headed back outside. 'I'm dying of thirst after all that trying on,' said Tasmin.

'Me too,' I agreed.

As we headed towards the nearest café, Tasmin

spotted a shop selling T-shirts. There were loads of examples in the window showing that the shop could personalise the design to whatever anyone wanted. I stood and stared for a few moments. 'I've just had a brilliant idea,' I said.

'Oh dear,' said Clover. 'Sometimes it's best to leave the country when someone has a *brilliant* idea.'

'So what's the idea, clever clogs?' asked Tasmin.

I pointed at the window. 'We have T-shirts made. One for each of us, with the front cover of *Songs for Sarah* on the front and the black-and-white photo on the back.'

'That is brilliant,' said Clover. 'We could wear them around Bath and see if anyone recognises it. Have you got the CD on you?'

I nodded. 'I've still got it in my bag from when I went to see FB. One small problem though. How am I going to pay for them?'

Tasmin looked in the window. 'They aren't that expensive. Three for fifteen quid. Bargain.'

We checked out purses. We had exactly nine pounds and forty pence between us. 'Enough to get a drink and a roll,' said Clover, 'and I'm starving. We can save up and come back and get the T-shirts done another day.'

'Or I could take the dress back,' said Tasmin but Clover gave her such a look that she quickly added, 'OK. OK, I'll keep the dress. It doesn't make sense to make another journey out here and pay our train fares again.' She looked around. 'OK, I've had another brilliant idea.'

Clover sighed. 'Lord help us. OK, let's hear it.'

'We busk.'

I burst out laughing. 'Yeah right.'

'Come on, killjoys. Both of you have studied drama. I know you can sing, Clover – in fact you've got a brilliant voice.'

We did everything we could to dissuade her but she wasn't having it and, ten minutes later, I found myself at the bottom of the hill, singing Christmas carols to passersby. We couldn't decide on any contemporary songs that we all knew the lyrics to. Carols were the only ones that we all knew. I decided to go with it and it got to be fun. When we started on 'Silent Night', I did a bit of mime too, to make it more of a performance. I'd done a class on it back in school in London and knew how to do the walking into a window mime with palms flat against an imaginary piece of glass. It cracked Tasmin and Clover up and they choked on their words.

Clover laid her jacket down as a make-do collection hat and a few people stood and watched for a couple of minutes, though most of them seemed to be laughing at us. It didn't put us off and luckily some of them chucked in a few coins when they drifted off. *If my class back in London could see me now*, I thought as I went into a rousing chorus of 'Ding Dong Merrily on High', *they'd think that Miss Straight and Sensible had lost the plot. Good, about time*, I told myself.

After about twenty minutes of going through our repertoire for the second time, an elderly man came forward and gave us a tenner. 'That's to shut up,' he said. 'It's May not December.'

'Thank you, I *love* you,' Tasmin called after him. We counted up our money and had enough to buy us all a drink *and* the T-shirts. Tasmin insisted on getting them made up so she took the coins needed and headed back to the T-shirt shop with the CD.

Clover pointed at the T-shirt shop. 'She'll try and bargain them down,' she said as we found a table outside a café halfway down the hill. We ordered apple juices then Clover texted her mum while I looked to see if Allegra had sent me a message. There wasn't one but there was a missed call from her. I hadn't heard it ring when we were in the shops.

Tasmin was soon back with our T-shirts and was already wearing hers. It looked great and when she turned around, there was the black-and-white photo on the back. 'And I got two quid knocked off too,' she said with a grin.

'We can wear them tomorrow for the Zoom festival,' said Clover.

'FB mentioned that. He's helping organise it,' I said. 'It was supposed to be a masked festival but no one was into it.'

'Good,' said Clover. 'Because I like to see people's faces properly.'

'Especially the boys,' said Tasmin. 'Bring your posh mate from London. Everyone will be there. Everyone – because everyone has a mate or a brother or a cousin who's in one of the bands. Loads of out-of-towners come as well. It's a fun day and someone's bound to see our T-shirts – who knows, even the elusive Sarah or her Mystery Boy?'

'Perfect,' I said.

Just as we set off for the station, my mobile rang. It was an indignant Allegra.

'Where have you been? Where are you? I've been trying for ages to get through to you,' she said. 'I've got so much to tell you.' And without asking if I could talk or not, she launched into her news. 'So Alex will be in Bath over the bank holiday. Something about a festival. Voom or Zoom.'

'Zoom. We were just talking about it. It's in the park near the Crescent. I thought we could go up there—'

'Ooh synchronicity. Love it. Where are you? I can hear traffic.'

'On my way to the train station in Frome,' I said as I watched Tasmin and Clover link arms and walk ahead so that I could chat in private. 'So Alex knows about Zoom?'

'Apparently. Said he goes every year. His cousin is a musician and is playing. Where's Frome?'

'Not far from Bath. It's got great vintage shops. And we've been busking.'

There was a silence on the other end of the phone . . . 'Are you on drugs?' asked Allegra finally.

'Just high on life,' I said. I was. It felt good and to top it all Alex was definitely coming to Bath. 'Everyone in Bath is a musician.'

'Sounds like you're included now. Anyway, he said to text him if we're going. He's given me his number.'

'Maybe he fancies *you*,' I said.

'No way. He specifically said he'd like to see *you*.'

'What exactly did he say? Word for word? What happened? Where did you see him? Did you bump into him or did he come looking for you? I need *details*, Allegra.'

Allegra laughed. 'OK. Let me remember. Details. I was in the car park after school last night, waiting for Mum, and he was there waiting for his ride. He saw me and came over. He asked if I'd heard from you. I said yes and that I was coming to see you over the bank holiday and he said, how amazing because he was going to Bath too. "Be nice to see her," he said. Then he asked were we going to that festival Voom—'

'Zoom,' I corrected.

'Zoom. I said I didn't know anything about it or what we were doing, then he said that if we weren't doing anything, it was worth going and that his cousin was playing. He said if we're going, we should text him and we can meet up. He gave me his number and then his ride came.'

'Are you sure he doesn't fancy you? Sounds to me like he was asking to see you.'

'He really wasn't, Paige. If he fancied me, he's had enough chances to ask me out and anyway, more importantly, one, he's not my type and two, you're my best friend and so it's hands off anyone you fancy.'

'I wouldn't stop you,' I said.

'Paige, shut up. I don't fancy Alex. Anyway, there will probably be loads of boys to meet at the Zoom festival. Bring it on, I say.'

When we finished our call, I ran to catch up with the girls. Alex coming to Bath. A music festival to go to. A mystery boy to find. Life was suddenly full of exciting possibilities. On the train home, I pressed play on my iPod. The track by Lady B started up again.

> Gotta get up, get out, get over it.
> Gonna put a smile on my face today.
> I just stepped into a brand new personality,
> Gonna beam out sunshine come what may.

Once again, *Songs for Sarah* was spot on in tune with me.

Chapter Nineteen

'We've hardly got started on the makeover so we have to finish it,' Clover insisted when we arrived back in Bath. 'All we've got is a dress for you, Tas, but Paige looks the same.'

'I don't feel the same,' I said and burst into a chorus of my favourite carol.

'We Three Kings of Orient are
Bearing gifts we traverse afar,
Field and fountain, moor and mountain
Following yonder star.'

Clover and Tasmin exchanged glances.

'Nutter,' said Tasmin.

'It was your idea,' I said and decided to treat them to the alternative version.

> 'We three salesman of Liverpool square,
> Selling nylons ten pence a pair.
> Some are plastic, some are elastic,
> Some aren't even fit to wear.'

Clover and Tasmin cracked up, then sang their version.

> 'We three Kings of Orient are,
> One in a taxi, two in car.
> One on a scooter, blowing his hooter,
> And following yonder star.'

'Nutters,' I said.

Clover and Tasmin bowed. 'Thank you,' said Tasmin. 'And welcome to the club.'

We got the bus up the hill to an area I hadn't been before called Bear Flat. Once off the bus, we headed up a steep road to Clover's house. It was a Victorian terrace with a small garden in front and great views down into the valley and Bath.

'You know Mum's a hairdresser and beautician,' said Clover. 'I texted her from Frome while you were in the T-shirt shop, Tas, and she's ready and waiting for both of you in the kitchen.'

'Sneaky you, and you never said anything,' said Tasmin. 'Well, she's not cutting my hair.'

'Or mine,' I said.

Clover threw her head back and did an evil mad-witch laugh. 'Mwah hah hah.' She beckoned us through the porch to the hall. 'Come into my lair, leettle girls.'

Tasmin rolled her eyes then pushed past her. 'Some days I despair about you, Clover Richards and you too now, Paige. Am I the only sane one here?'

'I won't answer that,' said Clover.

Her mum was ironing in the kitchen. She was tall, dark-skinned and as stunning-looking as Clover. She came and gave me a warm hug. 'You must be Paige. I've heard all about you,' she said. 'I'm Clover's mum.'

'Hi Mrs Richards,' I said.

'You can call me Sonia.'

She stood back and scrutinised my face and hair. She didn't say anything, then she turned to Tasmin and did the same. 'You first.' She looked at Clover and I. 'So girls, what's my brief?'

Clover made a motion to me with her hand as if to say, 'You say first.'

'I . . . ahem . . . OK, the brief is to do a make *under* on Tasmin rather than *over*. Make her look a bit more natural and maybe get rid of the hair extensions. Bit of gloss—'

Clover started laughing as she had done earlier when I made suggestions about how Tasmin could change her look. Sonia nodded. 'I get the picture. And for Paige, what do you think, girls?'

'Tart her up proper,' said Tasmin, then she laughed. 'I mean, a bit of make-up and—'

'Maybe a bit of a haircut,' Clover interrupted. 'It looks so heavy and she always wears it tied back.'

'Done,' said Sonia. 'Ok Tas, come with me.'

Tasmin sighed heavily then followed Sonia into a small conservatory at the back of the house where there was a salon area with a washbasin, and hair and beauty products on a silver trolley. Clover made us hot chocolates then we went into watch Sonia do her magic. And magic it was. Within minutes, Tasmin's extensions hit the bin.

'Yay!' Clover and I cheered each time her mum pulled one out.

Sonia laughed. 'I've been wanting to do that for ages.'

Tasmin looked shocked. 'Is there anyone who liked my hair extensions?'

'No,' said Clover.

Once the extensions were out, she shooed Clover and I away into the sitting room at the front. We flicked on the TV and chatted as we waited.

Half an hour later, Sonia came in.

'Ta-dah,' she said and opened the door for Tasmin to come in.

'Wow,' Clover and I exclaimed when she appeared. She looked amazing, softer and prettier.

She'd changed into her vintage dress and Sonia had done a great job on her hair. She'd trimmed off all the dead straggly ends, cut it straight just below her shoulders then blow-dried it so that it shone. The only make-up she had on was a slick of lip gloss, some blusher and mascara.

'Do you like it?' Clover asked her.

Tasmin shrugged but there was a glow about her and I could see that she was pleased with the result. She looked at me and raised an eyebrow. 'You next.'

I got up to go with Sonia and Tasmin flopped on the sofa.

'What would you like done, honey?' Sonia asked when we'd got into her home salon.

I sat in the chair she'd set up in front of a table laid

out with various items of make-up. 'I've no idea. I've always worn my hair this way.'

Sonia undid my ponytail so my hair fell over my shoulders. 'You have lovely hair but it's not really got any shape. How about I take a little of the length off and put in a few layers so that it falls better?'

'Um . . . OK.'

She started cutting and I felt slightly anxious when I saw hair falling onto the floor. Sonia must have seen that I was nervous. 'Just relax, hon,' she said. 'I moved the mirror so you don't watch and get freaked. Trust me. It's going to look great.'

Too late now, I thought as I looked at the dark tendrils of hair on the floor. *And she did make Tasmin look good.* After the cut, Sonia washed and blow-dried my hair then began to apply make-up to my face. It all felt very relaxing and as she brushed on shadows and applied foundation, I began to drift off, dreaming about vintage shops full of lace and velvet.

'OK, you're done,' said Sonia after a short while. She led me to the side of the conservatory where she'd put the mirror. 'What do you think?'

I looked at my reflection. She'd not cut as much off my hair as I thought but it looked different. She'd given me a side parting and graduated it from my jaw to the ends giving the shape style and movement. The make-up she'd applied was subtle, apart from a strong-red lip colour. It was me but not me. I looked sophisticated. 'I love it,' I said. 'I look like a grown-up.'

'You look beautiful,' said Sonia with a grin.

Clover and Tasmin came out and, when she saw me, Tasmin whistled. 'Look out, boys, there's a new girl in town. You look fab, cuz.'

'Good job, Mum,' said Clover.

'And you can have the make-up products,' said Sonia. 'I get sent samples all the time so they haven't cost me anything.'

'And there's more,' said Clover and started heading up the stairs. 'Come on up. I want to show you something.'

I followed her up to her bedroom with Tasmin not far behind me. Her room was colourful in reds, purple and oranges but it was so different to Tasmin's. It was neat and tidy with loads of magazines piled at the side of her bed. She went to her wardrobe and pulled out a petrol-blue bandage V-neck skater dress.

'Try it on,' she said.

'But I never wear dresses,' I said.

'Exactly,' said Clover.

I tried on the dress and stood back to look in the mirror. It fitted like a glove and looked fabulous.

'It's yours,' said Clover, who had gone back to rummage in her wardrobe. 'I got it from Topshop in the sale and it doesn't quite fit me. It looks as if it was made for you.' She pulled out a black bolero jacket. 'Put this on too.'

I did as I was told and the jacket looked great with the dress.

'Wear it tomorrow for Zoom,' said Paige. 'All the boys will be queuing up for you.'

I don't want boys queuing up for me, I thought. *Just Alex.* 'But I haven't got any money to give you,' I said.

Clover waved her hand as if dismissing what I'd said. 'I was going to take it to the charity shop. It's yours. You can buy me a coffee some time.'

I gave her a big hug.

'Lezzers,' said Tasmin, so I picked up a cushion from Clover's bed and biffed Tasmin with it. Clover soon joined in.

Tasmin grabbed the pillow from the bed. 'Don't mess with the professional,' she said and swung the pillow in the air then aimed it at Clover's back.

Clover soon retaliated. She leapt up onto her bed and took aim at both Tasmin and I. 'Pillow fight,' she called.

Soon we were all going at it, biffing and swiping. *So much for feeling sophisticated five minutes earlier*, I thought. It felt great to be acting like a kid and being mad. Tasmin was right. My style and personality came across as safe and sensible but that wasn't who I was inside. I was changing and felt like the real me was growing stronger. Who that was, I wasn't quite sure yet. Someone who wore a top hat and Victorian jacket in a vintage shop in Frome, someone who wore red lipstick or someone who could pack a mean punch when it came to the battle of the pillows?

When I set off down the hill later to go home, something at the back of my mind was nagging me, like an idea was trying to reveal itself. It had started as I'd been dozing at Clover's while her mum did the makeover – I'd been dreaming of vintage shops, velvet and lace, that had been it. I went over the day in my mind from the beginning – the train ride to Frome, the great vintage shops there, the dressing up, then the makeover. *People love dressing up in different guises, different costumes*, I thought as I reached the steps up to my new front door. Then ping. I had it. It felt like someone had just switched a light on in my head. I'd had the most brilliant idea! It was so obvious, staring me in the face all day. I took the stairs up to the flat two by two. I couldn't wait to tell Mum and Dad.

Chapter Twenty

'What is it, Paige?' asked Mum when I burst through the sitting-room door. 'You're all flushed. Has something happened? Your hair's been cut and you're wearing lipstick!'

'Yes, I had a makeover but it's not that,' I said. 'Something has happened. It's not bad. Nothing to worry about. Dad, I've had the most brilliant idea for your shop.'

Dad looked up from the television. 'OK . . .' he said.

I sat opposite them on the sofa and briefly noticed how cosy they'd made the room look. I told myself I'd have a proper look later. For now, I had important things to say. 'You've been trying to think of a gap in the market, yeah?'

Dad nodded.

'There's nothing like it in Bath – at least I don't think there is—'

'Like what, Paige?' asked Mum.

'And you could use your degree in costumes, Mum. You could make the costumes,' I blustered.

'Costumes for what?' asked Mum.

'Photo shop.'

Neither of them looked impressed and I realised I needed to be clearer. 'Not just a photo shop. More than that. Remember that time we went to Windsor and we went into that fancy dress shop and had our photos taken? Remember? Mum and I got dressed up as Victorian ladies and Dad, you dressed up as a gentleman with a false moustache and we had our photo taken.'

Dad still didn't look like he got what I was saying – he was staring out the window, seemingly lost in thought.

'Yes, I do remember,' said Mum. 'They had clothes from different eras.'

'Exactly,' I said. 'And here we are in one of the most beautiful heritage cities in England and there's nowhere like that for the tourists.'

Mum nodded but I wasn't sure she'd got the potential of my idea either.

'Everywhere you go in Bath,' I continued, 'people tell you about Jane Austen, that she lived here for a time, she set scenes in *Persuasion* and *Northanger Abbey* here. The whole architecture of the town is Georgian. You could get rails of clothes from the Georgian and Regency periods into your shop, maybe some Roman costumes too, set up changing rooms – you could even have the rooms styled in the old-fashioned way – and a photo area. People can come in, pick their costumes, have their pictures taken—'

'Maybe with a backdrop from the town? One of the crescents or an interior from the period? A fireplace and antique painting behind them?' Dad added. I sighed with relief. He'd caught on fast.

'Yes. And they would have a memento of the day,' I said. 'A great photo of themselves in period dress, the whole family, just like we did. What do you think?'

Mum looked over at Dad. 'I . . . I think it's a great idea. What do you think, Patrick?'

Dad got up. He was still looking thoughtful but then suddenly he broke into a wide grin. 'Paige, I believe you might be on to something here. It could work. Course we'd have to turn the photos round pretty fast so that people wouldn't have to wait long. That would be crucial but it could done.' He headed for the door. 'I'll just go and call Mike, see what he thinks, then check a few things online and do a few calculations.'

'And while the people wait, we could have some merchandise on sale,' said Mum. 'Cards, book markers, mementos, candles, ribbons.'

Dad came back in and gave me a bear hug. 'Paige, you little genius. You might just have saved our bacon!' He wandered back into the hall while he tried Uncle Mike's number.

Mum went over to her laptop which was on a table by the window. 'I'm going to check out Georgian costumes.'

'And Regency. It was visiting all the vintage shops in Frome that gave me the idea,' I said. 'People love dressing up.'

Dad came back in after speaking to Uncle Mike. 'I've left a message,' he said and sat at the table. 'Now. We need to do a business plan, research, a marketing plan.'

'And I'll design some backdrops, a logo, think about the interior of the shop.'

'And merchandise,' said Dad. 'We need to find out

where we can source the right stuff.' He sighed. 'All we need is the financing, so fingers crossed that Mike and Karen see the potential too.'

'They will,' I said, but neither of them were paying me any attention. They were both busy on their laptops researching online. I stood up and bowed. 'My work here is done.'

Once in my bedroom, I switched on my laptop and went to Facebook. I felt a shiver of anticipation when I saw that there was a private message from Alex. It didn't say much more than what Allegra had told me – that he was heading this way in the morning – but I felt such a rush of excitement. I went to his page, and in his comments space, he'd written: *Going to Bath to catch up with old friends and new.* I got the feeling I was one of the new.

I decided to scroll down his list of friends to see if I recognised any of the boys from the bands and sure enough there was Callum Casey. Another idea occurred to me. I could also look for Sarah's page. I kept on scrolling and then came to a profile photo that I recognised. 'Ohmigod!' I gasped and quickly grabbed my phone. I punched in Tasmin's number.

"Hey, sexy girl,' she said. 'Missing me already?'

'Yes. No. Whatever. Tas, you have to go to Facebook straight away. You'll never guess what I just saw on Alex Taylor's page. I was scrolling down looking at his friends—'

'Stalker.'

'I wasn't stalking him. Oh. Whatever. I was looking for Sarah's page too.'

'Good idea,' said Tasmin. 'Why didn't I think of that?'

'Tas, the photo was there. The black-and-white shot from the back cover of the CD. Someone was using it as their profile picture.'

'You're kidding? From *Songs for Sarah*?'

'Yes.'

'No way.'

'Did you check out the page?'

'I tried to. I couldn't get in. The privacy setting must be friends only. A message came up saying to see what he shares with friends, send him a friend request.'

'Bummer. Did you do that?'

'Not yet. I don't know if I want him to be able to know all about me, look at my page and so on when I don't even know who he is.'

'Could you see anything? Sometimes you can see quite a lot without being a friend. Does it say anything about school or work at the top?'

'I'm looking now. Ohmigod.'

'What?'

'In the About section, it says, lives in Bath. So he *is* from here.'

'Well we kind of knew that. Anything about school?'

'Nope.'

'OK, but you can see his friends even if he has privacy settings on. Click on his friends and see if there's anyone you know. See if there are any Sarahs. Also, are there any mutual friends?'

'Good idea. I'll have a look.'

'Call me if you see anyone we know.'

'Will do.'

I went back to the laptop and clicked on the boy's friends. Tasmin called me back a few moments later. 'I forgot to ask, what's his Facebook name?'

'That's what's really weird as well. It's Will.i.am Shakespeare. I don't think it's his real name.'

'Will.i.am as spelt like the musician from the Black Eyed Peas?'

'Exactly.'

Chapter Twenty-One

Mystery Boy

'You have witchcraft in your lips.'
Shakespeare: Henry V – Act 5, Scene 2.

We met, Sarah and I, completely by accident. I was up at the Royal Crescent for the Grand Regency promenade and the crowd of people dressed in the period get-up had just set off down to town. It was a hoot. Hundreds of them, probably boiling in the hot June weather. Men dressed as soldiers, others on old bikes with one wheel (penny farthings, I think they're called), women in long dresses and capes wearing bonnets and carrying parasols. It was like watching a film cast for a Jane Austen movie. When they'd moved off, I went with my mates to bag a place on the grass in the park and there we were, drinking cans and soaking up the sun when who comes by and spreads out a blanket next to ours? Sarah, with three of her mates.

Course we got chatting, all of us, about music, what schools we go to, what we'd seen in the Regency crowd. All having a laugh, though Ethan, Callum and Finn did most of the talking. She was friendly to all of us, not seeming to favour any one. I wondered if Ethan fancied her. Finn's got a girlfriend so he's not up for grabs and Callum's gay so he's not one to worry about either, though I wasn't sure whether she'd clocked it. Girls always like Cal. He likes them too, just doesn't fancy them.

'You the quiet mysterious one?' she asked after a while. I hadn't said much.

My first conversation with her and I couldn't think of what to say. 'That's me. Dark and mysterious.' It felt weird to be there, looking right into her eyes, the girl I'd fantasised about for weeks. She was even prettier close up, brown eyes in a heart-shaped face.

'I like your shades,' she said.

'Ta.' And I like you, I wanted to say but didn't. Girls don't like boys to be too keen. They like a challenge.

But at least she now knows my name and we're all meeting back here next week for the Zoom music festival. A casual arrangement, but is it more than that? Does she want to see me again? All my mates are in the bands that will be playing so it should be a good day. Will she recognise the music? Has she even listened to the CD? If she has, she'll know the tracks. Will she wonder if I'm there? The boy who made *Songs for Sarah*. I almost asked her. It was on the tip of my tongue but I resisted. *Hang back. Be cool*, I told myself. And next week, I'll see her again and can see how she reacts to the music in the park.

Chapter Twenty-Two

I went to meet Allegra from the train at ten-thirty the next morning. As I waited, I pulled out my sunglasses and put them on to hide the bags under my eyes.

I was feeling shattered because I'd spent half the night travelling the various mazes of people's Facebook friends. After I'd found Will.i.am on Alex's page, I looked at all his friends. There were loads of musicians there including Callum Casey, who was a mutual friend of both his and Alex's. In fact, they appeared to have a few mutual friends. I wondered if they actually knew each other or if, like so many of us, they have thousands of friends on their Facebook lists, some of whom are friends of friends or just at the same school, not real speak-to-every-day-text-every-hour friends. And so many Sarahs. It was such a popular name. The CD could have been made for any one of them.

It was frustrating looking at all the pages and not knowing who they really were. When Facebook first appeared, everyone at my old school added each other just because we could and it was like a competition to see who could get the most friends on their list. Only later did Allegra and I start to sift through and unfriend people we didn't actually know. Alex Taylor had a thousand friends. He couldn't possibly know them all, so might not actually know Will.i.am or whatever his real name was.

I made a note of the names of all the mutual friends that Alex had with FB and Will.i.am then went to their lists of friends and did the same.

Once I'd got started, it was addictive. Will.i.am Shakespeare showed up in a few of the lists of friends of friends. So did FB. He had added me as a friend the same day that we met so I could look at his page easily. I travelled down his lists. Alex was there and amazingly so was Niall Peterson. It appeared from the frequent comments from him that they were good mates. That surprised me. It didn't make sense – someone as nice and interesting as FB being a friend of Niall the knob.

I had a quick look on Niall's list of friends to see if Will.i.am was on there. He wasn't. I also made a note of all the Sarahs – there were eighty in total!

By about two a.m, I had lists and cross references to some different people. It seemed that most of the teenagers in Bath knew each other. I made a list of all those that I'd found with Will.i.am on their lists of friends and put it in my bag to take to the Zoom festival in the morning. There were too many Sarahs to write down and I didn't have the time in the end. If our plan A – walking around in the *Songs for Sarah* T-shirt – didn't work, my plan B was to try and find everyone on the Facebook list and ask if they actually knew who Will.i.am was. Clover and Tasmin might already know some of the names.

When I'd snuggled down into my duvet, I found it hard to sleep, even though it was late. I felt that I was getting close to finding out who the mystery CD maker was and it had occurred to me that he might even be Alex. It was possible. He had lived down here. And he still came down here regularly, and his cousin was a musician as well as the singer on track number one of the CD. So the likelihood of the boy I was looking for being Alex was completely plausible.

The London train was five minutes late but soon passengers were spilling out of Bath station into the square. Despite being tired, I had a really good feeling about the day – mates together in the park listening to good music, and maybe I might get closer to finding out who my mystery boy was. I took a quick look at the list in my bag, cross-referencing who knew who on Facebook. In the light of day, it made no sense at all – too many names and lines and squiggles – so I put it back in my bag. I stood on tiptoe to see if I could see Allegra, and there was she was coming through the turnstiles. She looked great as always. Her blonde hair tied back, dressed in skinny jeans and a white linen shirt and fabulous big sunglasses. Her face lit up when she saw me.

'Wow, you look amazing, different . . . more relaxed,' she said after giving me a bear hug. 'Bath agrees with you and I love the hair.'

I was wearing Clover's dress, the bolero jacket, a pair of denim blue Converses, my hair loose, and it felt good, like I was finding my style.

'You look great too,' I said, but secretly, I thought she looked a bit straight and safe. Probably how Tasmin viewed me when I arrived in Bath. Not that it mattered what Allegra dressed in. She was such a perfect English rose, she'd look good in a bin liner.

'Where's your mum?' I asked.

Allegra laughed. 'Driving down later. You know her. Couldn't get up. I didn't want to miss the music so she said I could come on the train. She's texted me about a million times already though to ask where I am? What time did I arrive? Double-checking that I call her later. She's on my case twenty-four seven.'

'Hi Paige,' said a male voice behind us.

'Hey, look who was in my carriage,' said Allegra.

It was Alex. I'd been so busy hugging my best friend that I hadn't noticed him standing behind us. I had to hang on to Allegra so that I didn't swoon. He was every bit as gorgeous as I remembered and looked genuinely pleased to see me. He came and gave me a hug too. 'Looking good, Juliet,' he said.

'You too, Romeo,' I said. 'How are the rehearsals going?'

He shrugged as we set off, crossed the road and headed up to town with streams of other visitors here for the day. 'Bit spaced out. People have got exams so there's not the focus that's really needed. And of course, we haven't got the right Juliet.'

Allegra punched him playfully. 'You smooth talker.'

Alex didn't take his eyes off me. 'I mean it.'

I know I blushed but it felt great to have to him look at me so intently and, unlike the old me, I held his gaze for a few moments. I know he felt a connection. So did I. *This new more confident me is definitely more fun*, I thought as I felt a tingling sensation that anything could happen.

We took the streets leading to the park. We chatted about school (he couldn't wait to leave and go to university), when he'd lived in Bath, (which was until Year Seven when his dad got a job in London), who he knew in Bath (loads of people, which I already knew from his Facebook page).

'And do you know a lot of musicians?' I asked.

'Yeah. You're probably finding this. Bath is like a big village. Everyone knows everyone, especially on the school circuit.'

'Do you know Callum Casey?' I asked, careful not to say that I already knew that he did. I didn't want to appear to know too much about him. That would be so not cool.

'Yeah. Do you know him?'

'I saw him play at Walcot Street. He's good. And I . . . I have a CD with one of his tracks on it.'

Alex smiled and looked pleased. 'One of his tracks?'

'Yes. The CD's a compilation but Callum's song is track one.' I scrutinised his face to gage his reaction.

He looked puzzled and hesitated for a few seconds before he asked. 'Compilation?'

'He didn't make it. Someone else did. It's on a CD called *Songs for Sarah*,' said Allegra.

Alex looked surprised. 'Sarah?'

'Yes. Does that ring a bell?' I asked still looking carefully at him.

Alex looked away. 'Not really.' I glanced at Allegra and shrugged. It was hard to tell whether he'd just happened to look away or was shocked that we knew about the CD and was trying to hide it.

'So how do you know Callum Casey?' asked Allegra.

'He's my cousin.'

'No way,' I said.

'Yes. I'll be staying with him. Don't tell me you fancy him? Most girls do.'

I decided that there was no harm in letting Alex know that he might have competition. I didn't want him thinking that I'd been just sitting about looking at pictures of him on the internet and waiting for him to come to visit Bath. 'He's good. I like his songs and he's cute.'

'And gay. So don't get your hopes up.'

That shut me up. So much for my make-Alex-a-bit-jealous tactic. I decided to forget being cool, just be myself and ask what I want to. 'I noticed that there was someone on your Facebook page who calls himself Will.i.am Shakespeare. Is that his real name?'

Alex looked blank. 'Will.i.am? I . . . I can't say I've noticed him. So you've been looking at my page?'

I wondered how to answer this. Whether to be honest or make a joke of it. I didn't want him to think I was obsessing over him so I decided to fill him in on the story and why I had been looking at his list of friends. I began to tell the story with Allegra joining in some of the bits she knew. When I'd finished, I pulled out the *Songs for Sarah* T-shirt. 'This is the CD on the front of the T-shirt and on the back is the black-and-white photo. That's the photo he uses as his profile photo and he uses the name Will.i.am Shakespeare.'

Alex's expression gave away nothing. It was hard to tell if he was bored by the story or deliberately keeping cool. I reminded myself that he was a good actor and could easily disguise what he was feeling. 'And why is it so important that you find this boy?' he asked.

'Don't tell me you're not intrigued,' said Allegra. 'I know I am.'

'Maybe,' he said. 'But what if you find the guy and he's a disappointment.'

I looked him straight in the eye. 'It depends on who he turns out to be.'

Alex raised an eyebrow. 'And what if he doesn't want to be found. What if the CD and all that went with it is history or a fantasy?'

Allegra nodded. 'Fair point, Paige. There has to be some reason that CD ended up in the charity shop. That's where people take unwanted items – emphasis on unwanted.'

'In a charity shop?' This time Alex couldn't disguise his shock but I wasn't sure whether that was because he was surprised to hear that's where the CD ended up or whether he had the snobby mentality that I used to have about second-hand things.

'Yes, That's where I got it,' I said. 'My aunt bought it for me.'

'I see,' said Alex. 'But sometimes I think you have to leave the past in the past and embrace what's in front of you.'

He looked right at me when he said that and again I felt that sweet sensation inside.

'Oh get a room,' said Allegra.

We both laughed, me more nervously than Alex, who seemed to enjoy the exchange. He put his hand on my arm. 'Seriously though, Paige, I wouldn't go about wearing the T-shirt. Not until you know more about what happened. Otherwise, you may be opening up old wounds for him and for her.'

I got the feeling he was talking from personal experience about a painful past. 'Did *you* make it?' I asked.

He raised an eyebrow again and smiled. 'Ah, that would be telling wouldn't it?'

'Oh come on, Alex, don't be a tease. If it's you, tell us.'

He grinned. 'And ruin a good mystery? No way. Anyway, I would have thought that if the CD really did speak to you then you would feel a connection when you find the boy who made it.' He gave me a meaningful look when he said the last part. There was no doubting that I was feeling a connection so why wouldn't he just admit it if it was him?

'You're being very annoying,' I said.

He grinned even more. 'Good. I like to know I'm causing a reaction.'

It *was* him. I just knew it. I had a million questions I wanted to ask. When did you make it? Who's Sarah?

Where is she now? But we'd reached the top of Milsom Street and Alex spotted Callum with his guitar outside a café. He went charging over and I was about to follow him when my phone bleeped that I had a text.

It was from FB. *Meet me to the right of the stage ASAP. Important info about your mystery boy. FB.*

I quickly texted back, *It's OK. I think I've found him. He's here.*

He texted back. *??? Not possible. He's here.*

I clicked my phone shut. 'Woah. Things are getting confusing,' I said to Allegra as I linked her arm and began to run towards the park.

Chapter Twenty-Three

Mystery Boy

Is this the generation of love? Hot blood, hot
thoughts and hot deeds? Why, they are vipers. Is
love a generation of vipers?
Shakespeare: *Troilus and Cressida* – Act 3, Scene 1.

Battle of the bands. Everyone was there. I looked for
Sarah in the crowd and saw her down the front. *Hang
back*, I told myself. *Hang back. Let her come to you.*
First Cybermentor played. I strained to see her reaction over the heads in front of me. As they started
playing, she turned to a friend to say something. Had
she recognised the song? I think she might have. It
was track eight on the CD. Overheated were on next.
They played track six. Then Lady B singing, Make
your life. A personal favourite of mine and was track

four on my CD. It was going like a dream. I couldn't have orchestrated it better. I edged forward. She turned and saw me, waved. I went to join her and asked her what she thought of the music.

'I'm blown away,' she said. 'I know most of it.'

'How?' I asked.

'It's from a CD,' she replied.

'What CD?' I asked acting cool.

'It was made specially for me,' she replied. 'Custom made.'

My heart stopped. 'Who by? And how do you know that?' I asked.

'He told me,' she replied.

That can't be, I thought.

'Sweetest thing anyone's ever done for me,' she said.

'Who is he?' I asked. 'Where is he?'

Sarah pointed. 'There he is,' she said.

I looked over the crowd to where she pointed. *Unbelievable*, I thought when I saw who it was. *The snake. I am going to kill him.*

Chapter Twenty-Four

From the throbbing bass notes resounding through the park, we could hear that the battle of the bands was underway.

Allegra was more interested in the beautiful Georgian architecture evident everywhere we looked. 'Ohmigod,' she said when we got up to the Royal Crescent and she saw the sweeping curve of the thirty tall houses towering over the parkland in front. They made an impressive sight. She pulled out her camera and starting taking photos. I couldn't blame her. I remember the first time I saw the Crescent and how blown away I was. I wanted to stay with her but I was also eager to find FB and see what he had to say.

'You go,' she said. 'Give me five minutes up here and I'll come and find you. Give me your T-shirt and I'll see if anyone recognises it.'

I pulled my *Songs for Sarah* T-shirt out of my bag and she put it on over her shirt. 'Well I'm not undressing in this weather,' she said when she saw me laugh. 'I wish I'd brought a coat!' In the twenty minutes it had taken to walk from town up to the park, the sky had grown overcast and looked like it might rain. 'Go on, you go,' she urged. 'See you in a minute.'

I followed the music and raced down through the trees to find the stage area where a band of four boys was finishing their set to rousing applause from the audience. I soon spotted FB, who was standing to the left of the stage. He waved when he saw me.

'So what's all this about you knowing who made the CD?' I panted when I'd got to him. 'Did you find another clue when you scanned the cover.'

He took a deep breath and hesitated as if unsure what to say. 'Not exactly. Nothing new anyway. I . . . I guess I should have told you . . .' he said. He stopped mid sentence when he saw a new performer get up onto the stage, his expression turning black. 'I don't believe it.'

'What is it? Do you know him?'

'I do. We all do. Keiron Mills. He's a creep.'

I looked back at the boy who was getting out his guitar. 'He looks familiar. I think I may have seen him somewhere, at school . . . around Bath . . .' I searched my mind to try and remember where it was.

'Probably playing in Bath. He busks a lot on the main drag near the Abbey,' said FB.

'That's it! I knew I'd seen him somewhere. It was on my first day here. He was playing in the square next to the Abbey and this idiot who lives next door to Tasmin was heckling him.' I suddenly remembered that I'd seen Niall's name on FB's list of Facebook friends. 'Oh! Sorry. I think you know him. Niall Peterson. He was giving Keiron a really hard time.'

'Niall? Good,' said FB. 'Someone needed to.'

'Why? What's he done?'

'What hasn't he done? Keiron's trouble. He nicks people's material and lyrics, changes a few things ever so slightly and then passes them off as his own. He's notorious for it, as well as being a liar. He might look sweet-faced but he's got no morals at all. It's an unspoken rule amongst musicians: you don't steal other people's material. He does – he changes a few words here and there but everyone knows that he does it.'

'So that's why Niall was giving him a hard time. I thought he was just being mean.'

FB shook his head. 'Niall? Nah. He hasn't got a mean bone in his body. He's a good mate.'

'Maybe for boys but he's a player when it comes to girls.'

FB looked shocked. 'Niall? I doubt it. I've known him a long time and know where he's at. He's one of the good guys. What makes you think he's a player?'

'I saw him with three girls in one day.'

FB laughed. 'Girls like Niall. No doubt about that, but that doesn't make him a player. When was this?'

'When I first arrived in Bath. First there was a blonde one, then a redhead, then I saw him in town with his arm around a girl with short hair.'

'Chestnut coloured?'

I nodded.

'OK, she's his friend, Carol. Just mates. He's known her forever. The blonde is his ex. She follows him around like a puppy dog and chances are, if you saw them kissing, actually it was her kissing him. She's always turning up begging him to go back with her. The redhead was his new girlfriend. Was. She didn't last long. She was still hung up on her old boyfriend and went back to him. So back to the drawing board.'

'He seems a bit full of himself too.'

FB laughed. 'Not really. He's been a good friend to

me, especially last year when I was down when my dad was ill. He's the kind of guy who'd do anything for a mate. And Niall's not a player, I do know that. He's a bit of a romantic in fact. Looking for The One he says, but then aren't we all?'

I felt a fool. I remembered Niall telling me that things weren't always as they seemed. Having heard what FB had said about Keiron, I realised that I'd jumped to conclusions and judged Niall. *He must think I'm a first-class bitch*, I thought. I owed him an apology.

Up on the stage, Keiron started playing and there was cheering from the crowd and some booing. 'See what I mean,' said FB. 'Niall isn't the only one who doesn't like him. I can't believe his cheek actually, getting up there in front of the very people he's stolen from. But forget him for a moment, what did you mean, you'd found the boy who made the CD?'

'Yes. Well I think I have. I'm pretty sure it's my friend from London. I think he might be one of your Facebook friends too, though I looked at so many last night that I can't remember who knows who. I've got a list somewhere, though it doesn't make as much sense today as it did last night. Anyway, it doesn't matter any more because I'm sure it's Alex.'

'Alex? From your old school? No. It can't be,' said FB.

'Why not?' I asked.

'Did he say for certain it was him?'

'Not exactly but he intimated that it was.'

FB shook his head again. 'He's messing with your head.'

'How do you know that?' I asked again. 'And what was it that you wanted to say to me about the boy who made it.'

'Oh . . . just to keep an open mind,' said FB.

'Meaning what?'

'He could be anywhere, be anybody,' he continued.

'Well I already know that.'

'Could even be me!' FB blurted. 'Have you considered that?'

I burst out laughing, then saw that FB looked hurt. 'What's so funny?'

'You'd have said so when we first made the announcement that we were looking for the boy who made the CD.'

'Maybe I wanted to get to know you first.'

'OK. Then who's Sarah?'

FB looked like he'd gone into a sulk. 'Sarah might not be real,' he said.

'Not real?'

'Maybe she's a fantasy girl. Someone who was made up. Or maybe she is real and I do know who she is but the Sarah the CD was made for was . . . she's a fantasy Sarah.'

I sighed. 'What are you on about? This really isn't funny, FB. I thought you and I were friends, and you know what this CD means to me, so why are you winding me up like this? Now I don't know what to think.'

'I'm not winding you up, honest. I just wanted to say that you should keep an open mind and don't pin too many hopes on when you find the boy, that he's Mr Perfect. We know what the CD is about – meeting the perfect girl – but what about if it's not like that in real life. Maybe you're looking for a fantasy boy more than a real one with flaws. That's all I wanted to say. Try and see what's in front of you instead of avoiding relationships by holding on to a romantic ideal.'

Inwardly, I felt myself squirm. It felt like FB had seen right inside of me. Mystery Boy was my fantasy, the dream I escaped to when I was feeling low or feeling full of self doubt, a place where everything was perfect, but I didn't want to let FB know how insightful he'd been. 'Wow. That's heavy stuff, FB. What are you really trying to say?'

'I'm trying to say that I think we have something special regardless of whether I made the CD or not. We have so much in common.'

'We do—'

'I know I'm not Mr Hunky Gorgeous like, say, Niall,' FB interrupted.

'He is not gorgeous, or at least he might be but he's not my type. He's so obviously good-looking. I prefer someone more interesting.'

'That's what I thought,' said FB. 'That's why I thought I could risk telling you how I felt. You wouldn't throw it back at me.'

'I . . . I . . .' I felt totally confused and glanced away. I noticed Alex coming down over the park towards us. He was with Callum and he waved when he saw us then pointed towards the stage, then at Callum, as if to say that he was going to go with his cousin. I gave him the thumbs-up to say I understood.

FB's expression looked even sulkier. 'Your Alex is Alex Taylor?'

'Yes. How do you know him?' I asked.

'He used to live in Bath. We went to the same junior school. He wasn't one of my mates and we stay in touch on Facebook. He's your Alex?'

'Well not *my* Alex exactly.'

FB looked at me closely and then back over at Alex's back. His expression said everything. 'But you'd like him to be,' he said wistfully.

Our conversation was interrupted by the arrival of Clover and Tasmin who were both wearing their *Songs for Sarah* T-shirts. FB looked shocked when he saw them.

'Where's yours?' asked Tasmin. Her face was slightly flushed and she smelt of alcohol.

'Allegra's got it on,' I said.

Clover nodded. 'Where is she?'

'Taking photos at the Crescent,' I said and looked at droves of teenagers who were still arriving in the park, many now carrying umbrellas to keep off the rain that had started.

'What's the idea?' FB asked. 'You never told me about the T-shirts.'

'And why should we?' slurred Tasmin. 'Since when do we need your permission?'

I was about to tell her that Alex and FB had both insinuated that they were the mystery boy when FB blurted, 'because I've been helping Paige find him too.'

'But—' I started.

'So far no luck,' said FB and shot me a warning

glance as if to say don't tell what we'd been talking about. What was he playing at? I wondered.

'We're going to listen to the music,' said Tasmin and started to go over to the area where people were seated on the grass. I noticed that she was swaying slightly as she tottered away. 'You coming?'

'In a mo,' I said. 'Er . . . has there been any reaction to the T-shirt?'

'Loads,' said Clover. 'People think they're really cool. A few people have asked where they can get one. We should get a market stall selling them. Catch you laters.'

As soon as they were out of earshot, I turned back to FB. 'What is going on FB? If you are Mystery Boy, why can't I tell them?'

'Why do you think you haven't found out who he is. Maybe he wants to be anonymous. Say it is me. No one would know who I am. It's like wearing a mask and people can't make fun or assumptions.'

'But how do I really know if it's you or Alex?' I asked.

FB looked deeply into my eyes. 'In the same way that I know it's really you. You're the girl I've dreamt about but this time, you're real. Don't be like me, Paige, hiding in a fantasy because you're afraid you may get hurt. Make it real.'

I felt totally conflicted and confused. Alex had said something similar, that I'd know when I met the boy. I liked FB but I'd never thought about him as boyfriend material. He was my friend – but we did get on well. I could talk to him more easily than any other boy I'd ever met. Why shouldn't I think of him as a boyfriend? *Because there just isn't the chemistry*, I thought. *There isn't. When I look into his eyes I don't feel that flutter. But how do you tell a boy that you don't fancy him?* I asked myself. The last thing I wanted to do was hurt his feelings. *How can I tread on his dreams?* Suddenly it made sense that it could be FB. I understood. A boy like him wasn't the obvious babe magnet like Niall or Alex. Making a CD like *Songs for Sarah* was a way for him to express his deepest feelings without being known or rejected. It made sense that if it was him, he would want to stay anonymous, but then he'd just made himself vulnerable by revealing his feelings about me. *God, this is difficult*, I thought.

'But you hardly know me, FB–' I started, but FB put up his hand, palm facing me.

'Don't,' he said. 'And don't give me the "can't we be friends" line either.'

'But–' I began again.

'In love there are no buts,' said FB and he turned and walked away.

I felt awful, mean and cruel, but mostly frustrated. 'Wuh-arghhhh,' I muttered. I turned and kicked the nearest tree just as Niall Peterson walked into sight. He glanced at me then at the tree. He didn't say anything. Not a word. He just walked on by.

For a nano-second, I thought about going after him, to apologise for judging him, to explain why I was kicking a tree. *And how is that conversation going to go? I asked myself. Oh yes, I always kick trees that have done me no harm. No point. Now he probably thinks I'm bad tempered as well as a judgmental grumpy bitch.*

'You OK?' asked Allegra, suddenly appearing at my side.

'Boys do your head in,' I replied just as the skies opened and it began to really pelt down. Not the usual soft Somerset drizzle, this was like a tropical storm that soaked everything and everyone in seconds. As we made a dash for cover, I thought, *This day is so not turning out the way I'd planned.*

Chapter Twenty-Five

My frustration about boys soon vaporised with a new concern. Tasmin. By late afternoon, everyone had taken shelter in the refreshment tents and piles of teenagers were packed in there like sardines. The air smelt musty from damp clothes and hot bodies, and the noise level was high with so many people talking or shouting to make themselves heard. Vodka bottles and alcopops were being quietly passed around and just outside the tents, under the trees, there was a smoking area, but I knew the groups out there weren't just smoking roll-ups or cigarettes. I recognised the smell of weed from parties with sixth formers that I'd been to in London.

I found Tasmin at the back of the pizza tent. She was slumped on the floor at the end of the counter and she wasn't alone – a few of her mates from school were with her, including Clover. They all seemed to be out of it, talking loudly slurring their words, some of them being clumsy, falling over or bumping into each other. At first it was all a laugh and they were funny to watch but as time went on, I noticed that Tasmin was responding less and less.

'How much has she actually drunk?' I asked Stu.

Stu shrugged. 'Dunno. Same as most of us. She'll be fine. Chill, Paige. Have a drink yourself.'

Clover offered me the bottle of vodka to which she'd added cranberry juice. I didn't really like alcohol but I took a swig because I didn't want her or their mates to think I was uncool. It tasted sour to me. Allegra had no qualms about refusing the bottle. 'You don't know who's been drinking from it,' she said.

I'm not prudish about alcohol nor is she. It was just that we'd been to enough parties in London and seen people acting like idiots or throwing up, particularly boys, to show us that it wasn't always that much fun.

'I'm worried about Tasmin,' I said. 'I've never seen her like this and think she may have overdone it.'

Allegra went over to check her out. She tried to rouse her but Tasmin hardly opened her eyes. She was well gone. 'Let's go and find Alex,' she said. 'He'll know what to do but I'm sure she'll be fine. She's just pissed.'

We found Alex outside the tent with all the stoners. It had stopped raining, though the clouds above were still dark and threatening. There was a large group of boys passing round joints and Alex was in the middle of them. He appeared to be very happy and very stoned, his eyes heavy and bloodshot.

'Hey Juliet,' he said when he saw me.

'I'm worried about my cousin,' I said and filled him in on her condition.

He put his arm around me, 'Paigie, my little Julietie. I think you worry too much. Worry, worry. Have a smoke and chill. Your cousin's probably fine. It's you we need to worry about. Miss Safe and Sensible.'

What he said hit a nerve. Being seen as safe and sensible was so not what I wanted to be and I thought I'd left that persona behind, but it wasn't me to swig back the vodka and get stoned. It didn't appeal. Maybe I *was* safe and sensible, despite the makeover and new clothes. Maybe I had to accept that. I wriggled out from his arm while, over on the stage, a band began to play and the stoners, including Alex, turned to listen. He was soon moving in time to the music, arms waving above his head and I, and my anxiety, had been forgotten.

'I don't know what to do,' I said to Allegra.

She glanced back inside the tent. 'Pizza,' she said. 'Maybe she needs to eat something. I'll go and get some food, you go and check on her. Having something to eat might help soak up some of the alcohol she's drunk.'

Back inside the tent, Tasmin was still unresponsive but everyone around her seemed unconcerned and were chatting away as if it was completely normal to have someone in the group passed out in front of them. Maybe I'd overreacted. I decided to try and make the most of the rest of the afternoon, listen to the music and enjoy what I could of it. Allegra was still at the end of the pizza counter in a long queue. She was talking to someone. I stood on tiptoe to see better. It was Niall Peterson. He glanced over at me so I looked out of the tent flap then back at him and gave him a shrug as if to say, 'Rotten weather, isn't it?' He looked blank. He clearly didn't speak shrug language. I decided to go over and apologise for my behaviour when I first met him.

'Hi Niall. Er . . . when I first met you, er . . . I know now that I got the wrong end of things and er . . . after that too. I want to say I'm sorry.'

222

'Sorry for what?' asked Allegra.

'Getting the wrong end of the stick,' I said. 'I acted like a total idiot when I first met Niall.'

Niall shrugged a shoulder as though he couldn't care less. 'No problem,' he said then pointed at the drinks at the other end of the counter. 'I'll go and get us some juices – to go with the pizza – then my mate FB's band is playing.' He looked at me intently. 'I believe you know him.'

'Yes. Yes I do and I'd like to see him play too. How did you know that we know each other?'

'Word gets around,' he said, then headed off to get drinks.

When he'd gone, Allegra quickly turned to me, 'He's a bit dreamy, isn't he? And you actually know him. How come you never mentioned him?'

'I don't really know him. I er . . . he lives next door to Tasmin.'

'Would you mind if I get to know him?' she asked.

'Course not. Why would I?'

'I thought I sensed some chemistry between you.'

'Chemistry? No way. Honestly, we hardly know each other and the only encounters we've had have been a bit er . . . weird.'

'Why?'

'Oh just me seeing something that wasn't there. I saw him heckling some guy and I thought he was being mean but turns out the guy had stolen some people's music.'

'That's not cool.'

'No. But I didn't know that at the time. Anyway, yes, course. Niall, you. Go for it.'

'OK. Great. I didn't think you'd mind. You have enough boys to be interested in with Alex, FB and Mystery Boy. Niall seems really nice. He was asking about the T-shirt so I told him a bit about the CD and the mystery boy. I'm surprised you haven't got to know him better.'

Too late now, I thought. *He hates me.*

When Niall came back with the drinks, I felt even more confused. To my surprise, I felt a flicker of jealousy when I saw Allegra flirting with him. Clearly, I did mind that she wanted to get to know him. It was Alex I fancied, wasn't it? But seeing him outside the tent had shown me another side of him and not one I was sure I liked.

As we squeezed ourselves into a space on the floor and tucked into the pizza, I noticed that, over in the corner, Tasmin still hadn't stirred. I wondered whether to try and wake her and see if she wanted to eat anything. Niall followed my gaze to where she lay sleeping.

'Tas?' he asked, as if he'd read my thoughts and knew that I was worried about her.

'Yes. I don't know if I should be worried or not. It's probably just me being my usual boring sensible self. I guess she just needs to sleep it off.'

'Maybe,' said Niall. 'Would you like me to go and check on her?'

'I think I would, if you don't mind. Just, she looked a bit pale before, blue almost, and her breathing seemed slow.'

'Blue?' asked Niall. He looked alarmed, got up immediately and went over to the other side of the tent. Two minutes later, he called me over.

'Is she OK?' I asked.

'I think she needs help,' he replied.

'You do?'

He nodded.

'What like black coffee or something?'

'Not black coffee,' he said. 'Sorry it's me being the bore here but I did a class about this after a mate of mine got seriously ill. I think she's in danger of getting alcohol poisoning.'

I felt myself starting to panic. 'What does that mean? What do we do?'

'There's a first-aid ambulance parked further down the field,' he said. 'I'll go and alert them.'

'Do you want me to come with you?'

He shook his head. 'No. You stay here. Wake her up. She won't like it but keep her conscious. Make sure she doesn't fall asleep or pass out again. Turn her on her side and keep her warm. Use your jacket or something – borrow one from someone if you need to. Think you can do that?'

'Yes, yes, course. And . . . do you think it would help if she threw up?'

'Not necessarily. She's not in control and we don't want her to choke.'

He ran out of the tent and Allegra and I did our best to rouse Tasmin, but she didn't respond. I looked around for Clover but couldn't see her. I felt myself getting alarmed and by now a few people were staring. What if something happened to her? I cursed myself for not trusting my gut feelings earlier. I knew something wasn't right. 'Tasmin, Tasmin, wake up,' I urged as I tried to rouse her. She didn't even stir.

Five minutes later, Niall was back with two ambulance men carrying a stretcher.

'Jesus,' said one of the men as he looked around at the pile of teenagers then back at his colleague. 'Think there might be more than one who's overdone it.'

He rolled his eyes. 'They never learn, do they?'

Moments later, Tasmin was carried out and everyone stared. A few of the stoned boys cheered as she was carried past and, at last, Clover appeared. The sight of her friend lying comatose on the stretcher seemed to sober her up fast. 'Is she going to be all right?' she asked.

'I don't know. I'm going to go with them,' I replied as I pushed through the crowd to the ambulance that was parked outside the tent where a crowd had gathered.

Niall was at the back of the ambulance and he came over when he saw me. 'They said we did the right thing,' he said. 'They're going to take her to the hospital. Do you want to go with her?'

'Yes. Of course.'

I climbed into the back of the ambulance with her just as Allegra appeared. 'Shall I come too?'

'It's not a party,' said one of the medical team. He turned to me. 'Do you know who this person is? And where she lives?'

I nodded. 'I do. She's my cousin.' I turned to Allegra. 'I'm so sorry but can you stay here? I'll call you as soon as I can.'

'Don't worry. I'll look after her,' said Niall as Allegra looked up at him coyly. 'Let us know how she is.'

'I will.' The ambulance men closed the doors and as we drove off I held Tasmin's hand. *Can this day get any worse?* I thought as the driver turned his siren on and we picked up speed. I felt utterly confused.

So much had happened so fast. Alex, FB, Niall. I realised I hardly knew Alex at all. Was he my mystery boy or just winding me up? I'd projected so much on to him and now it appeared he was a stoner who liked to mess with girls' heads. And then there was FB. I thought I'd found a friend for life, but was that going to be possible if I didn't return his romantic feelings? Could he be the mystery boy who'd made the CD? If he was, I couldn't help it, but the thought made me feel disappointed. It made me realise how much I had staked in finding whoever had made the CD. What an expectation I'd had. And finally Niall. He was turning out not to be the person I'd thought he was either, but in a good way. In fact, he'd turned out to be a bit of a hero.

Maybe it's me, I thought. *I am just a rubbish judge of people. I got Alex wrong and I got Niall wrong.*

I realised that one of the ambulance men was staring at me. 'Rough day, love?' he asked.

Sudden tears pricked my eyes. 'You could say that,' I replied.

Chapter Twenty-Six

Mystery Boy

'Loving goes by haps; some Cupid kills with arrows, some with traps.'

Shakespeare: *Much Ado About Nothing*
– Act 3, Scene 1.

People lie about who they are. I found out who he was. The tosser who claimed he'd made my CD. It wasn't hard. Some idiot from Weston Park school. Keiron Mills. He's well known around here for stealing people's music, changing it a bit then passing it off as his own. I found him. I decked him and Sarah flew at me saying I was a bully. 'He's a liar,' I said.

'You're weird and you're jealous,' she said.

I left. I've been a fool. She's not The One. She got the music but she didn't get me.

I went back to her and Keiron. She had her arms round him and he was playing along like he'd been really hurt, but I hadn't hit him that hard. 'I'd like my CD back,' I said to her.

'Is your name Sarah?' she asked.

'No,' I said.

'So it's not your CD,' she said. 'Now get lost, loser.'

At home, I cursed myself. I'd projected perfection onto her. My fantasy girl, but I'd never even spoken to her. How could I know what she was really like? Lesson learnt. I shan't do that again. Next time, I'll take time. Get to know a girl before I give my heart. What a waste. She's not The One. I was mistaken.

Chapter Twenty-Seven

'What's happened?' asked Allegra on my mobile a couple of hours later.

'I'm just leaving the hospital,' I said. 'Aunt Karen and Uncle Mike arrived a while ago and are with Tasmin now.'

'How is she?'

'She's regained consciousness. They pumped her stomach and now they're rehydrating her.'

'Woah, that's intense. But honestly, what an idiot,' said Allegra. 'Why do they do it? I mean, I have a drink every now and again, but why do people drink to oblivion.'

I laughed. 'You're sounding like your mum again, Allegra.'

'Am I? God. But hell, you know what I mean.'

'I do. My aunt and uncle looked as bad as Tasmin when they got here. Well freaked out, and pale and sick with worry, though the young doctor that had been tending Tas assured them that she was going to be all right. I felt really sorry for them. They didn't know whether to be mad with Tas or cry with relief all over her.'

'And are you OK?'

'Yeah. I feel a bit drained that's all. And I'm sorry about abandoning you the first time you come down to Bath.'

'No problem. Niall looked after me well. Your mate FB was pissed off that you didn't see his band play, by the way.'

'Oh you met him too? You explained, didn't you?'

'Yes. He understood. That boy has an almighty crush on you.'

'I know. I don't know what to do about it.'

'Shame you don't like him. He's a sweetheart.'

'I know and I hope we can stay friends. I really do value him but just don't fancy him. Are you still with Niall?'

'No. I'm back at the hotel with Mum. It's *très chic*. Do you want to come here for a while?'

'I'm just about to get on the bus,' I said. 'It goes

233

from right outside the hospital and stops almost outside our front door. Do you mind if I just go home and see you in the morning?'

'You sound a bit low.'

'I just hate hospitals. The smell. The heat. It's full of sick people and it was awful seeing Tasmin like she was. I was so worried something serious had happened.'

'They'll look after her.'

'Shall I come over to you in the morning?'

'No, I'll meet you in town somewhere. Mum's doing the Spa and I said I'd meet Niall and FB. I could text Alex as well if you like.'

'Maybe not Alex. I might feel differently tomorrow but I'm not sure I want to see him at the moment. I don't know how I feel about him any more. He . . . I don't think he's who I thought he was.'

'I understand. He was out of it, wasn't he? Stoners can be so boring as boyfriends. Remember that guy, Ian, I went out with last year? As soon as he'd had a smoke, it was like someone had taken his battery out. All he wanted to do was sit around. Not a lot of fun. OK. Laters, Paige.'

'Laters,' I said as a bus drew up, opened its doors and I hopped on.

*

When I got home, I was glad that Mum and Dad were out. Dad had texted me earlier that they were going out for a meal to talk over ideas for the fancy-dress photo shop. No doubt they'd get to hear all about the day soon enough and I'd have to face the inquisition about Tasmin and whether I'd been drinking too. For now though, all was quiet and there was something I wanted to do – and that was to message Will.i.am. Alex and FB had both hinted that they made the CD but only the boy who really made it would have had access to the black-and-white shot used as the profile photo of Will.i.am.

I went into my room and switched on my laptop. I was about to send Will.i.am a friend request, when I thought, *No, I don't know for certain who he is so if I send him a message, why should he know who it's from.* I clicked out of my page and onto the link to create a new Facebook profile. I would be as anonymous and mysterious as he was. There was a file full of photos of masks on my desktop so I used a beautiful ornate black-and-silver Venetian one for my profile shot. I found Will.i.am's page and sent a friend request. I got an adrenalin rush when I saw that he added me immediately. He was online!

I quickly typed a message. *Missing person alert. Seen today on T-shirts at the Zoom festival. Who is the boy in the black-and-white photo on the back of the CD Songs for Sarah?*

There was a ping. A reply in the box at the bottom right-hand side of my page. *I saw three girls at the Zoom festival with my photo on the back of their T-shirt. Which one were you?*

I typed back. *None of them. I didn't wear the T-shirt.*

What do you want?

To know who you are.

Why?

I can relate to the tracks on the CD, I typed.

You like it?

Yes.

I made it a while ago. All ancient history.

What happened? I asked. It felt amazing to be finally talking to my mystery boy. I just needed to find out which of the boys I suspected he was.

Love is a smoke and is made with the fume of sighs, he replied.

I knew that line! *Romeo and Juliet, Act 1, Scene 1.* I typed.

Impressed, he typed back. *You know your Shakespeare. Who are you?*

Who are you? I replied.

I will tell you but not yet.

Where is Sarah?

I told you. She's ancient history.

I wasn't going to give up. All my and Tasmin's attempts to find Sarah on school lists in Bath had failed. No girls had recognised the CD cover on the T-shirts and come forward at the Zoom festival, but maybe she'd been doing something else this weekend. If I knew who she was, I could contact her, maybe on Facebook too, and ask her who had made the CD.

Yes but where is she?

College in London. She left Bath last September.

Hah. So that's why Tasmin, Clover and I couldn't find her.

When will you tell me who you are?

When I know more about you, he wrote back.

Not fair, I typed then I took a deep breath. Time for the new more confident Paige to come forward, I thought. *Meet me tomorrow at Society Café in Kingsmead Square.*

You're fast. How do you know I am in Bath?

I don't but I bet anything you are. Two boys said they made the CD. Which one are you?

Two boys?

Yes.

Interesting.

Not really, I typed back. *It's confusing.*

I might not be either of them.

Yes but you might. Will you be there tomorrow?

Maybe.

Good. Meet you there at midday.

How will I know you? he asked.

I will carry your CD. How will I know you?

He didn't reply to that and I could see that a moment later he'd gone offline. I was sure he'd be there tomorrow. A date. I was buzzing with anticipation. It felt good to have made a positive move. While I was at the hospital, I'd thought a lot about what FB had said to me earlier in the day. Was I pinning too much on finding out who my mystery boy was? My expectations too high? Was I comfortable to have a fantasy relationship where I couldn't get hurt? No. I was sure I wasn't. I'd show him it wasn't like that.

I wanted Mystery Boy to be real. I wanted to meet him and find out once and for all if it was fate that I found the CD that day in the charity shop and all that had happened had been leading me to him. I wanted to find out if there could be anything between us or not.

I switched off my laptop, sat back in my chair and had to laugh. I'd found him but my mystery boy was more of a mystery than ever. *Not for much longer though*, I told myself.

Chapter Twenty-Eight

I got to Society Café at five past midday on Monday. I was on my own because Allegra's mum had booked Allegra a massage at their hotel and she never could resist the chance to be pampered. She'd texted that she'd see me later.

When I entered the café, I noticed that there was a family upstairs on one table and a girl in the corner reading a book. There was no sign of any boys so I made my way across the floor and down the stairs to the basement area.

Halfway down, I could see that two of the tables were occupied. one by a couple. At the other was a boy. He had his back to me but I knew without him turning around that it was FB and a wave of disappointment flooded through me. I hesitated on the stairs. I hoped he wouldn't hear me so that I could turn and go. It felt cowardly but what would I say to him? Hi FB, so you are the mystery boy, but too bad because I don't fancy you? I turned to go back up when I heard the café door open and footsteps head across the floor and towards the stairs. A moment later, Alex appeared.

'Paige,' he said, then grinned. 'I thought I might bump into you again today.'

'You *did?*' I said. I felt surprised because I had almost eliminated the possibility that he could be Mystery Boy. 'And why would that be?' If he was my mystery boy then I wanted him to say it.

On hearing the sounds of our voices, FB turned around. He looked surprised to see Alex and I. 'Hey,' he said. 'You're both here.'

I went down the steps and over to him. 'What are you doing here?'

FB laughed then pointed at his cappuccino. 'Coffee. This is a coffee shop.'

'I meant, are you meeting anyone here?'

'Yeah. You two,' he replied as Alex sat next to him on the bench and I sat opposite.

'Hey,' said Alex to FB.

'I mean had you *planned* to meet anyone here?' I asked FB.

He looked perplexed. 'It's pretty loose but I usually always see someone in here. So an unplanned plan.'

Grrr, I thought. *Why can't anyone just say what they mean? If he's Mystery Boy, why doesn't he say in plain English? Or is he holding back because Alex is here?*

Just at that moment there were more footsteps on the floor above us. Someone else was crossing the café then clattering down the steps. We all looked up to see who it was. This time it was Niall. He glanced over at the three of us then rolled his eyes.

'Can I join you?' he asked. 'Or is this a private party?'

Alex shifted over on the bench he was sitting on to make room for him. 'Not at all, come and sit with us.'

Niall squeezed in then glanced over at me. I looked from his face to Alex's to FB's. All three were staring at me, grinning. I didn't grin back. A niggling thought had entered the back of my mind and was bothering me.

'Is this a coincidence or did the three of you plan this?' I asked.

The three of them looked at each other as if they had no idea what I was talking about. If they were acting, they were doing a good job.

'Plan what?' asked FB.

'This meeting,' I replied.

'I hadn't planned to see anyone in particular,' said Alex.

'But then you always bump into someone you know in here, don't you?' said Niall.

FB nodded. 'Just what I said,' said FB. 'Sort of casual plan.'

I wasn't totally sure, but I felt that they were having a laugh at my expense. If they were, I wasn't finding it funny. 'OK. Which one of you calls himself Will.i.am on Facebook and made the CD *Songs for Sarah*?'

'Ah . . . You thought you were meeting *him* here, didn't you?' asked FB.

'I did and now I don't know what to think. Which one of you is it?'

'Me,' said FB.

'*No*. It's me,' said Alex.

Niall sighed. 'No, it's *me*.'

I let out a long breath. 'I don't believe it. Why are you doing this?'

Alex shrugged. 'It's a CD, Paige. No big deal. If I made it, so what? I've made loads of CD compilations.'

'Me too,' said FB.

'Me too,' said Niall.

'But this was special,' I said.

'Why?' chorused the three of them.

'I've told you all. Don't you get it? It's because, whoever made it, I have a lot in common with him. We'd get on. I know we would.'

'Then it was definitely me,' said Alex with a nod to the other boys. 'I'm Will.i.am.'

'You mean me,' said FB.

'It *was* me,' said Niall. 'I'm Will.i.am.'

It wasn't my imagination. They were having a laugh, egging each other on in the way that boys do when there are few of them.

'So funny,' I said. 'Go on then, wind me up, have a laugh, but I think it's mean of you.' I got up and ran back upstairs and out of the café. I stepped out and took a deep breath of fresh air. *I am going to forget all about this*, I thought as I crossed the square. *It's doing my head in.*

'Paige,' I heard someone call behind me.

I turned to see that Niall had followed me out of the café. I stopped and he came over. 'You OK?'

'No. You were all laughing at me.'

'I'm sorry.' He shrugged. 'I don't think any of us meant to upset you. I certainly didn't. But does it matter so much? Does it matter who made your CD? Surely what matters is who you want to be with, spend time with. You. What do you want?'

'I want to know who put the tracks together.'

Niall nodded. 'OK. It was me *and* FB—'

'No, don't start that again.'

'No, it's true. It was both of us. It was my idea but I asked FB to help. He knows so much about music. I told him what I wanted to express so he put some tracks together for me to listen to, but I chose them and did the artwork.'

I stared at him and he stared back. No laughter this time. He appeared to be telling the truth.

'So does that mean you have to choose between us?' he asked.

I ignored his question. 'What about Alex? Did he have anything to do with it?'

Niall shook his head. 'He was just messing about in there. Having a laugh. Not to wind you up – just it was kind of a Spartacus moment.'

'Spartacus moment?'

'Yeah. The film. Spartacus, played by Kirk Douglas.

245

He led the slave uprising against the Romans in the movie. There's a moment when the slaves are captured and the Roman general demands that Spartacus is handed over or all the slaves will be executed. He comes forward and says, "I'm Spartacus". Behind him another man steps forward and says, "No, I'm Spartacus", then another, then another, until there are thousands of them all saying, "I'm Spartacus." It's actually quite a moving moment.'

I considered his explanation. 'Hmm. I see what you mean then. I hope I don't get thousands of boys all claiming to be Mystery Boy, three of you are enough.'

Niall laughed. 'Yeah. I guess that could be confusing but I doubt that's going to happen.'

'So were you hoping that Sarah would fall in love with you or was it FB who was in love with her?

'No, it was me. FB said his contribution to the CD was to a sort of fantasy girl that he hoped to meet some day. He took finding the right tracks as a project. For me, the girl was real, or sort of real.'

I nodded. So FB had been telling the truth or half of it. I remembered that he had said that whoever made the CD had good taste in music. I hadn't suspected for a moment that he'd helped choose the tracks!

'What do you mean, sort of real? What happened with the real Sarah?' I asked.

'It didn't work out. She wasn't who I thought she was. What I mean is, she was real but I projected a lot on to her. It was all in my head. The perfect girl. So it wasn't real. Do you know what I mean? Do I sound mad?'

I thought of Alex and shook my head. 'I do know what you mean, exactly,' I said.

'She couldn't possibly live up to my expectations,' Niall continued. 'No girl could so Sarah was a kind of fantasy girl. I didn't know the real her until we spoke to each other and then it became clear very fast that she wasn't who I'd imagined she was. Big lesson for me not to project on to people until you've got to know them. So, as I say, it didn't work out and she's ancient history.'

When he said that, I knew he was the boy I'd been chatting to on Facebook last night. He'd said Sarah was ancient history too.

'She's not even in Bath any more. She went off to college somewhere.'

'So why didn't you say it was you earlier?' I asked. 'You must have known that I was looking for you.'

Niall nodded. 'I did. Right from the first day at the music festival on Walcot Street. FB texted straight away about it, though to begin with we weren't totally sure whether it was you or Tasmin who was looking for me. I hoped it was you. I didn't say anything because I wanted you to get to know me first, for me. Then that went AWOL because it appeared that you hated me.'

'And you hated me.'

Niall smiled. 'Not exactly. I really liked that you loved the music and the idea behind it. And it was intriguing seeing what you did. The T-shirts etc. I planted a clue too by opening the Will.i.am Facebook page weeks ago. I had copies of the CD cover on my computer so it was easy. And you found me on there in the end but it got me thinking. Why is this girl looking for me with such determination? Is she looking for some fantasy boy or a real one? A bit like I did with Sarah. It worried me. You've thought about this mystery boy for so long, the one who made your perfect CD. What if he's not all you hope for?' For a brief moment, Niall looked vulnerable.

I looked into his eyes. 'Only one way to find out,' I said. 'Spend time with the main contender.'

Niall smiled, a lovely warm smile that lit up his face. I could see why he had a queue of girls after him. 'Sounds good to me,' he said as I spotted Allegra appear on the other side of the square. She waved when she saw us. My heart sank. Allegra. My best friend. She liked Niall and I had said I didn't mind if she pursued him. *Why oh why is love so complicated?* I asked myself as she crossed the square to come and join us.

Little Miss Gooseberry. That's me. I have totally blown it, I thought as I trailed around town after Allegra and Niall. They seem to have hit it off perfectly, laughing at each other's jokes, enthusing over shared interests. 'Oh me too!' Allegra exclaimed when Niall said he liked action movies. 'Me too,' Niall said when Allegra said she liked acoustic music. 'I love that band,' he said when she mentioned one of her favourites.

I tried to make an exit at one point and leave them to it. I didn't want to appear insensitive to the fact that love was blossoming in front of my eyes and I might be in the way, but neither of them would hear of it. Plus I needed time alone to work out what was happening to me. I felt a strong attraction to Niall and I was pretty sure that he'd felt it too when we'd looked into each other's eyes outside the café. Was he just being charming to Allegra? Or was he, as I'd first thought, a player and stringing us both along? When

FB had said he was one of the good guys, it might have just been FB defending his mate.

'Allegra is only down for such a short time,' said Niall when I offered to give them some space. 'I wouldn't dream of encroaching on your time together. It should be me who goes.'

'Yes,' said Allegra. 'Don't go, Paige. I didn't see much of you yesterday and I have to be back at the hotel at four because Mum wants to head back to London. Please don't go.'

'But Tasmin's home now,' I said. 'I thought I'd visit and check she's OK.'

Niall waved his hand. 'I saw her mum this morning. She said she's doing fine and will be home this afternoon. I'll check in on her later. One thing I can be sure of though and that is that Tasmin won't be that bothered if she has visitors or not. She's probably nursing a very sore head in a darkened room.'

'I guess. And having to put up with the wrath of both her parents,' I added.

'Yes,' said Allegra. 'She ruined enough of yesterday. Let's not let her spoil today as well.'

We decided to head down to Southgate where there was an afternoon of dance performances from local schools scheduled on the fake lawn area in the middle of the shops. Loads of people hang out there on deck chairs when the weather's good. On the way over, my phone bleeped that I had a message. It was from FB.

Sry about b4 and hope we didn't upset U. Just wanted 2 say that I may not be The One but I'd like to be one of the people in ur life. XXX

It was a sweet message and I did hope that we could be friends and that he wouldn't want anything more. Only time would tell that.

In the meantime, Niall proved to be good company and interesting to talk to as we walked down through town. And he laughed easily. I liked that. I couldn't cope with a moody boy. But he clearly fancies Allegra, I told myself when we found some empty deck chairs in the open paved area outside Debenhams and flopped down into them. Niall was in the middle between Allegra and I, and my chair was positioned slightly behind so, when the first dance act started, I was able to observe Niall without him seeing. Great profile, straight nose, long eyelashes.

I got the CD out of my bag, studied the cover and then his profile. It was him. Definitely. His face was blurred on the photo underneath the strips of paper which were stuck down like prison bars but yes, it was him. *Why hadn't I seen it before?* I asked myself. I wanted to ask him so much about why he'd chosen the images he'd used? Did he feel like he was in a prison when it came to love? I certainly did. Today anyway. Trapped with feelings inside that I can't express. I turned the CD over and looked at the black-and-white photo. Yes. Now Niall was in front of me, I could see the shape of the boy silhouetted against the window was exactly his stature and shape. FB was chunkier and Alex had wider shoulders. I wanted to ask where the photo was taken when he suddenly turned around. 'I can feel you staring at me,' he said.

I immediately blushed bright red. 'I wasn't.'

'You were. I could *feel* it,' he replied. The way he spoke to me was urgent, as if he was feeling a lot more than me just staring at him. I felt a bolt of electricity pass between us.

Allegra glanced round, first at me, then at Niall, then back at me. She doesn't miss anything and her eyes narrowed. Niall took a deep breath, held my gaze for another few seconds then turned back to watch the dancers. *Woah. That was intense*, I thought as I felt my inside melt in response to Niall's look. Allegra was still watching me, her expression questioning. A few moments later, she got out her phone and began to text. My phone bleeped that I had a message. *What's going on?* she'd typed.

No idea, I typed back. *Never been so confused in my life.*

Want me to butt out? she typed. *I can see he's into you.*

No way. He's into you.

Wake up and smell the hormones, Paige. Niall fancies you. Mind you, so do Alex and FB. Gd job I am going back to London. My confidence couldn't take much more of this. Then she did a smiley face to show she wasn't upset.

Niall glanced around and down at my phone then at Allegra and her phone. He didn't miss anything either.

Chapter Twenty-Nine

Mystery Boy

I knew straight away that this girl was special, though we got off on the wrong foot. I saw her in town and there was something about her. Dark glossy hair, eyes bright with curiosity, taking it all in. She took an instant dislike to me. Hah. Apparently some girls do. They either love me or hate me. Like Marmite. But things are getting better. I'm drawn to her. She occupies my thoughts and I think of things I'd like to tell her. Places I'd like to show her. Does she know how I feel? Does she care or feel the same way? I need to get to know her better. Not like before when I was so wrong about Sarah. I didn't know her at all. This girl is different. There's more to her and I want to get to know everything about her. But what to do? I need to make a gesture to let her know that she's got to me. But what?

Chapter Thirty

Alex sent me an email after he'd gone back to London.

Dear Paige

I felt that there was something between us from that first day when I turned and saw you were to be Juliet. I was sad when I heard you were leaving but then given hope when I discovered you were moving to my old stomping ground, Bath. I visit often to see my cousin. But I saw that I have competition. The path of love never did run smooth. I'm sorry if I messed with your head that day in the café and at the Zoom festival by saying I made the CD. I didn't, but you were so fixated on finding whoever did that I thought I needed to create a diversion. Get in there and fight for you. All is fair in love and war etc . . . All I can say is, you know where I am. CD or no CD, you have to choose who you want to be with. I'll be down your way again at the end of June for the Regency Parade. I hope things are clearer for you then.

Yours, Alex

I called Allegra to ask what she thought.

'Only a few weeks ago, I'd have felt flattered, over the moon, but when I read his email, all I felt was pressure. I like Alex, course I do, or did. As you know, I've had a crush on him forever.' *Niall's and FB's words of wisdom about projecting on to someone seem to apply more to Alex than either of them*, I thought. In my head, I'd made Alex into the perfect boy and then felt let down when I found out he was a stoner and he wasn't there for me when Tasmin was taken to hospital. 'But I realise now I don't know him at all.'

'Press alert,' said Allegra. 'I've been asking around about Mr Perfect and it appears that he's not. I think you were starting to realise that anyway.'

'So what have you found out?'

'He's Mr Charm personified and he uses that to get off with as many girls as he can. I saw him chatting up loads of different ones at the Zoom festival – that's when he wasn't too stoned to stand – and there's a whole list of girls here at school who were wooed, won then dumped once he'd made his conquest. Although that might be because he's looking for the right one, which might be you. What does your gut tell you?'

It wasn't Alex's face that came to mind, it was Niall's, but I reminded myself that I didn't really know him that well either. 'To take my time. I've been so obsessed with the CD and finding the mystery boy and now we know it was two boys, Niall and FB. And I also feel confused because I genuinely did feel chemistry with Alex and now I do with Niall too. How can I feel attracted to two boys?'

'There will probably always be chemistry with different boys but knowing which ones are good for you and which bad for you is part of growing up, I think.'

'I guess. I–'

'You don't have to make your mind up right now. It will become clear in time. Just leave it. Maybe hang out with Niall and FB. Email Alex. See what happens.'

'You are very wise, my blonde airhead friend.'

'I know,' said Allegra. 'Just call me Alleguru. Oh, and Paige, if you see FB, tell him I said hi.'

Hi to FB? I thought when we'd finished our call. *Interesting . . .*

Over the following few weeks I spent time with FB and our friendship was as comfy as ever. He got that we weren't going to be a love affair and seemed happy to just be mates especially since I'd passed Allegra's message on. They'd been texting and emailing and made a plan to meet up next time she was in Bath, which according to her would be soon. When I told Mum and Dad about FB's amazing masks, they asked him to make some Georgian ones for the shop, which he agreed to do. He didn't mention the CD again and nor did I. It was as if we'd both made the decision to put it behind us and move on.

Niall had clearly come to a similar decision and took his Will.i.am page off Facebook. He added me as a friend to his Niall page though and we often chatted online after school. It was as if we'd both decided to give each other another chance and get to know each other better. I found out that he was studying art at A level so it was great to be able to talk to him about it as well as FB. I even found out that the mate that had made the Shakespearian masks on FB's wall had been Niall and so we were able to talk about those too.

Most nights there would be some message from him, sometimes a quote or a poem or a link to a piece of music or painting. In turn, I sent him things that I'd seen or heard that I liked. I told him all about my art project and he sent me loads of links to portraits. He suggested that the three of us, FB, him and me, went out some time taking photographs of people that I could work on. He also told me that he was doing exams and hoped to go to college to do graphic design. I told him he'd be good at designing books, CD or DVD covers. That was the only allusion I ever made to *Songs For Sarah* though I still listened to the song tracks. It would always be a favourite.

At the weekends I often saw Niall and FB at the usual hang-out places when I went to meet Tasmin and Clover in town or down by the canal. Like with FB, my relationship with Niall was growing into a friendship and I found him easy to talk to because he listened to what I had to say as well as talked about what he was into, unlike some boys who only like to talk about themselves. I was also finding myself increasingly attracted to him. Sadly, I wasn't the only one. He always seemed to have girls hanging round him, though I couldn't see that there was anyone special. Tasmin had recovered from the alcohol scare and had sworn off the stuff for life, though Clover teased her and said never say never about anything, a conclusion I had come to about boys.

FB and I would often see each other after school. I helped him with some of the masks he was making for the shop and it felt good to have a shared purpose – though the masks weren't the only thing we had to talk about. He took every opportunity to ask about Allegra. They had clearly hit it off at the Zoom festival and I couldn't think of anyone more perfect for him.

I'd catch Niall looking at me occasionally but he always looked away before I felt the lovely warm feeling that had passed between us at the Zoom festival. I started to wonder if he just wanted to be friends, in the same way that I just wanted to be friends with FB. *Love is hard*, I thought, especially as in the last week, there appeared to be a new girl hanging out with our crowd and whenever I saw Niall in town, she was there too.

Molly Myers. Dark glossy hair, same colour as mine. She went to Prior Park College and was really cool and funny. Apparently they'd got off to a bad start too when they first met but had got to know each other since. Niall always seemed to be laughing when he was with her. I wanted to ask Tasmin to find out what was happening but she'd probably say something to blow my cover so I kept my mouth shut. I knew that boys liked a challenge and to do the chasing so I didn't want Niall to know that my feelings for him were growing. If I'd had any doubts about him, the spark of jealousy that I felt when Molly showed up made things mega clear to me. I liked him a *lot*. But I wanted him to choose me. So many girls seemed to go for him. I wanted to be different. I just hoped that it wasn't too late and Molly Myers and he weren't going to become an item.

Mum and Dad had wasted no time getting the new business up and running. On the last Friday in June, Allegra came to stay and after meeting her at the train station, we went into town to see how the shop was shaping up.

'Awesome,' I said as I looked around. The last time I'd seen the space, it was an empty shell with no colour or character. Since then, while I'd been out at school, Mum and Dad had been busy. The main room had been decorated in typical Georgian fashion, complete with fireplace and heavy old curtains that Mum had sourced on ebay, plus huge gilt mirrors from a shop in town that did house clearances. They'd also found furniture, lamps and paintings from the same period to make the room look more cosy. 'It's like stepping back in time. You've done a great job. It's exactly what people come to Bath for.'

Dad nodded. 'I think we're about ready for the opening tomorrow.'

I felt so good as I took it all in – proud of Mum and Dad but also that it had been my idea. On one side there was a rail of costumes, some that Mum had made, others she'd sourced in vintage shops or on ebay with Clover's help. On the other side there was a counter and area set up for the photographer. Dad had been interviewing all week and had come up with three employees, two men and one woman, who were to take the photos.

Allegra and I had a great time going through the rails to pick our costumes for the Regency Parade, which was happening the following morning. She mentioned that Alex had said he might come for the weekend but I no longer cared about him. I'd moved on.

FB came to meet us and it was obvious that he and Allegra wanted to be alone for a while so I made up some excuse about having to do something at the shop for Dad so that they could go off for a while on their own.

At first, Dad had dismissed the idea of opening the shop on the same day, saying everyone would be in fancy dress so why would they come in the shop? Mum'd talked him round though telling him that lots of people would see crowds walking around Bath in costume and be inspired to take part so when they came across the shop, they'd come in, try on costumes, get their photo taken and feel part of the day. The plan was that Tasmin, Allegra, Clover and I were going to go out with flyers to advertise. We'd be dressed up in period costume too, though Tasmin balked at the idea at first. She relented when Dad offered to pay her. In the evening, there was to be a ball and banquet at the Guild Hall. Half of Bath would be attending and Mum and Dad had booked a table for us all. It was going to be a top day and I felt a buzz of excitement just thinking about it.

Chapter Thirty-One

Allegra and I were up early in the morning to go and walk about, Regency style. She was as excited as I was about the day but more because she'd be meeting up with FB again than about the Parade. 'He's the first boy I've met in ages that doesn't play games and is straight about how he feels. I like that.'

I was as pleased as she was – two of my favourite people together.

Tasmin and Clover came over around nine and after coffees and croissants, we got dressed in the costumes that Mum had brought home for us the night before.

'Uck,' said Tasmin when she saw her reflection in the mirror. She looked so sweet and girlie in a white

265

muslin dress with pink ribbons. She immediately hoiked the long skirt up on one side and tucked it in her knickers. She added a pair of sunglasses, a slick of red lipstick then looked in the mirror again. 'That's better. I reckon I could start a trend. Sort of post-Austen punk.' She did look great and had made the outfit look cool, plus she hadn't gone back to the heavy make-up she wore before her makeunder.

Allegra looked like she had just stepped out of a BBC costume drama in her pale blue dress, matching bonnet and soft curls. 'The perfect English rose,' I said.

'Thorny and has mildew,' she replied with a laugh. I knew she was joking – she knew she looked the business.

'You look like a proper lady of the times,' said Clover. She managed to look exotic even in Regency dress. She wore a short scarlet jacket that fastened just under the bust on top of a long olive-green dress, and a red bonnet with green feathers and a scarlet parasol.

My dress was honey coloured with a plum-coloured cape over it and Mum had found me some matching velvet slippers. I put my hair up in a comb at the back and looked in the mirror. A girl from another time stared back at me.

'You look good,' said Tasmin. 'It suits you.'

'What? Prim and proper?'

'No. Actually I think you look sophisticated and interesting,' she replied.

Clover acted faint. 'A compliment from Tasmin. Press alert.'

Tasmin replied by making a rude gesture with her fingers.

'Ever the lady,' said Clover.

We set off for town in bright sunshine and any shyness we felt soon disappeared when we saw other people dressed in costume. It was as if we'd somehow stepped into a time machine and gone back to another era.

'The location lends itself to people dressing from the period,' said Allegra as a tall handsome boy in a velvet coat and knee-high leather boots walked past. He saw us looking at him and bowed like an old-fashioned gentleman.

We all curtsied back except for Tasmin who rolled her eyes and then popped a piece of gum into her mouth.

'So unladylike,' said Clover.

'Whatever,' said Tasmin then winked at the boy.

While the girls were busy eyeing up the boy talent in the crowds, I popped into the shop to collect our flyers. Mum and Dad had been there since early morning and looked handsome in their Regency dress, Mum in peacock blue and Dad in dress coat and cravat.

'You both look great,' I said. 'Romantic.'

They grinned back at me. 'Just get those customers coming this way,' said Dad.

'Hand the flyers out to everyone,' said Mum as she passed the heavy bag of leaflets.

'She means everyone not already in costume,' Dad added.

'Don't worry, we will,' I assured her. *The sooner we get rid of this weight, the better*, I thought as I went out to join the others. I divided up the leaflets for them, then we headed over to the Pump Room where the parade was to start.

There were hundreds of people there: old, young, men on penny-farthing bicycles, boys dressed as soldiers in red regimental uniforms, others in long coats and top hats. The women in empire-line dresses with short jackets on top, bonnets, feathers and hats, some with pretty parasols, some with fans, most with their hair up with ringlets at the side. The sun was shining, it was an amazing spectacle and everyone seemed in the best of moods as they noted and commented on each other's choice of dress.

'I feel like I'm on a film set,' said Clover as she looked around.

'I feel like we've gone back in time,' I said.

'Sexy,' said Allegra as we watched another boy walk past. With shoulder-length black hair, dress coat and the high leather-boots typical of the period, he looked really good.

'So much more romantic than modern dress. I think we should dress this way all the time,' said Clover.

'For puke's sake,' said Tasmin. 'No way.'

We weren't the only ones who had noticed the boy. As he made his way through the square he was frequently stopped and asked to pose for photographs with various women and girls. Allegra and I had both brought our cameras so we spent the next hour partly doing our job and handing out leaflets, which were disappearing fast, and partly posing for photos with each other or people from the crowd, or when we saw a good backdrop like one of the Georgian terraces or cobbled streets.

As we walked up to the Royal Crescent, we saw lots of people we knew from school – some boys watching the parade but not participating, a few dressed up with family or friends, loads of girls who dressed up like us. I spotted Niall in the crowd ahead of us. He looked so handsome, dressed similarly to the boy we'd seen earlier in the square, in calf-length brown velvet coat and high leather knee-boots. On his arm was Molly, who looked lovely in an apple-green dress and bonnet. She was looking up at him and he was smiling at something she'd said. I watched as a group of three girls, also in costume, went over to join them and they took turns having their photos taken.

I felt a stab of jealousy as I watched him put his arm around Molly's shoulder for one of the shots. They made a perfect-looking couple. He hadn't noticed me so, feeling like a sad stalker, I made myself turn away and go back to the girls, who had targeted a group of tourists and were handing out the last of the leaflets and giving directions to the shop. I could see that Mum and Dad were going to be busy.

'Do you think we should go and get more leaflets?' I asked after I'd handed out the last one to a little Japanese lady.

'Not yet,' said Tasmin. 'Let's go and have some fun.'

Clover nodded. 'I've sent so many people down to the shop that they'll be maxed out, so yeah, I'm with Tasmin – let's go and have some fun.'

I glanced ahead to see if I could still see Niall but he'd disappeared into the crowd. *I have to let it go*, I told myself. I didn't want seeing Niall with Molly to ruin the day as it did hurt that it wasn't me he was with. Although Tasmin had told me that I was naive when it came to boys, there was one thing I did know and that was that if a boy was interested, he wouldn't go swanning off with someone else on his arm.

I looked around me. The sun was still shining and Bath, with its honey-coloured stone, had never looked more picturesque. As I looked over at Clover and Tasmin, chatting away and doing crazy faces for the camera, I reminded myself how things had changed since I'd first arrived. I had a lot to be happy about. To my right was Allegra, my old friend, and to my left, my new friends, Tasmin and Clover. All my worry about the distance between Allegra and I going to different schools hadn't changed things between us one jot. Within minutes of seeing each other, we were right back where we always were. Boys. *Who needs them?* I told myself as I got my camera out to take more photos.

In the evening, we took seats at our table for the banquet in the Guild Hall. The dinner and dance were to take place in a vast tall room decorated in cream and pale green where enormous chandeliers sparkled down from the ceiling. There were long tables set with tablecloths and flowers, and a stage at the far end where a group of musicians were playing violins. I recognised loads of faces we'd seen earlier on the parade but no sign of Niall.

At our table were Mum and Dad, Aunt Karen and Uncle Mike, Jake, Joe and Simon, all dressed in period costume, though the boys didn't look too happy about it, and Allegra, Clover, Tasmin and I. We'd had the most brilliant day just walking about the city watching what was going on and I'd taken some great photos. My favourites were of Tasmin dressed in her costume tucking into a McDonald's and smearing ketchup up her cheek, and another of FB (who was in costume) and Allegra doing their version of Regency dance in the middle of Milsom Street. FB had come to help us distribute leaflets but I suspect he had an ulterior motive, which was to spend more time with Allegra.

Mum and Dad were in a great mood, having had a successful day at the shop.

'If every day is like this, I think we have ourselves a business,' said Dad, his face beaming. 'We didn't stop at all from first thing this morning.'

'No reason why it shouldn't be,' said Uncle Mike. 'Tourists arrive daily by the train and coach load and you're well placed to attract them in.'

'And we have so many ideas for developing things,' said Mum. 'Once we get the feel of it, we can expand into more merchandise and maybe even a café area so people can have a drink while they wait for their photos.'

I saw her look over at Dad and smile at him. I felt a lurch of happiness. Everything was going to be OK. The sadness that we'd felt when we left London now seemed like ancient history. As soon as I thought that, I remembered Niall's words about Sarah. Ancient history. I wondered where he was, who with and what he was doing. *Mustn't think about him,* I told myself. *He's clearly not interested and I'm not going to let a boy ruin the day.*

After a fabulous dinner of salmon, new potatoes and asparagus followed by strawberry mousse and shortcake, more musicians joined the others on the stage and people began to line the hall ready to dance. When the music started, it seemed as if they all knew the steps from time gone by. I was transfixed as I watched them gracefully move around the room and it felt like we really had gone back a couple of centuries.

'I bet Jane Austen even came and danced here,' said Allegra, picking up on my thoughts. 'All we need now is a couple of Darcys.'

'Just one would do,' I said. 'I've had enough of complications.'

Mum, Dad, Aunt Karen and Uncle Mike got up to dance and, after watching them for a while, Tasmin leant over.

'They've set up a hall downstairs for some local bands to play. Want to go?' she asked.

'In a while,' I said. I already knew that there would be music downstairs because FB had texted Allegra to say that his band would be playing at nine o'clock and that we must be there. In the meantime, I was enjoying watching the dancing so much I didn't want to miss a minute of it. I did scan the room again to see if there was any sign of Niall amongst the diners and dancers but there was none. I felt disappointed that I hadn't heard from him and he hadn't even come looking for me to say hi. Curiously, I wasn't bothered that Alex hadn't been in touch and wasn't even sure that he'd come down from London as Allegra had said.

Allegra and Clover went with Tasmin so, when it got close to nine o'clock, I went downstairs to find them.

The hall on the ground floor couldn't have been more in contrast to upstairs. It was disco city, full of teenagers, and up on the stage FB and his band were belting it out.

I looked for my friends and saw them on the dance floor, all with their long skirts tucked in their knickers *à la* Tasmin's version of Austen style. Clover and Allegra were still wearing their bonnets, as were a number of girls. It was a funny sight to see all the girls in long dresses boogieing away, and one boy in the corner in his dress coat and boots was doing a moon walk much to the amusement of his mates.

Allegra saw me and waved so I went over to join them. We danced through a few numbers and I noticed Alex to my right with his arms around a petite blonde girl. So he had come down. *Well, he didn't waste any time*, I thought. *So much for his email saying how much he wanted to see me next time he's here. He didn't even text me to let me know he was here.* As I watched him, I felt relieved that I hadn't got too involved and then had my heart broken when I realised, as I inevitably would, that I was just another name on his list of conquests.

FB's band finished their set and FB took the mike. He looked over the audience and when he spotted me, he nodded. 'And now we're going to slow the pace down a little and to do so, we have a guest performer. Let's hear it for Niall Peterson.'

Clover, Tasmin, Allegra and I all glanced at each other in surprise.

'Niall?' said Tasmin. 'I didn't know he sang.'

'Me neither,' I said.

'Our mystery boy has hidden talents,' said Clover.

'Maybe,' said Tasmin. 'We haven't heard him sing yet.'

Niall came out centre stage. He was still dressed in the velvet coat and high knee-breeches. He looked slightly nervous as he scanned the audience, as though looking for someone. I looked around too, expecting to see Molly, and there she was on the opposite side of the room. My heart sank when I saw Niall give her a nod of acknowledgement. He was going to sing to her. But no, he was still scanning the audience. A moment later, he saw me. He made himself stand taller, took a deep breath and smiled. 'OK, this next song is for a very special person here tonight.' He glanced behind at FB and gave him a nod and FB began to play his guitar. After a few chords, Niall began to sing, looking straight at me while he sang the lyrics. He had a great voice, mellow with a lovely rich tone.

It's you.

Not just mates, more than dates, we're soulmates.

No matter what they say I know today's the day

to stick my head above the parapet.

There is no other word for it.

It must be love.

It's you.

I've been acting like a fool, breaking all the rules.

Now I take my heart from my sleeve

and ask you please, to believe

In a thing called love.

Tasmin nudged me. 'He's singing to you. Way to go Niall,' she whispered.

He can't be, I thought as I looked for Molly again, and there she was listening along with everyone else. 'He can't be,' I said. 'He's been hanging out with Molly.'

'That's as may be,' said Tasmin, 'but he's singing to you.'

I looked back at the stage where Niall was still watching me and directing all the lyrics to me.

It's *you* . . .

I admit I was lonely, make me your one and only.

Want to hold you close and say,
When I saw you that first day,
I knew . . . it was love.'

As Niall continued to look at me, I surrendered myself to the moment. I knew I was blushing and that half the audience was looking to see who Niall was singing to. It didn't matter. I didn't care. It felt amazing. I felt connected by an invisible thread to Niall and for the rest of his song, it felt like we were alone in the hall.

'This *is* for you,' whispered Allegra.

I didn't take my eyes away from Niall. 'I know,' I said. It was the most romantic moment of my life. *This song could have been for Sarah if things had worked out differently*, I thought. *But fate led me to find the CD that day in the charity shop, then inspired my search for the boy who had made it, and then to this moment here. And there he is, my mystery boy no more, smiling down at me. Your loss, Sarah, wherever you are.* FB played a few more chords, Niall took a bow and the audience cheered.

'That was *so* cool,' said Clover as we watched Niall leave the stage. Then FB's band went into another number.

'Go and talk to him,' said Allegra and she pushed me in the direction of the stage.

'I . . .' I didn't need to move because I saw Niall come out into the crowd and look for me. I went straight over to him. 'Thank you, that was—'

I couldn't get any more words out because Niall grabbed my hand and pulled me towards the door.

'Where are we going? I asked.

'Somewhere private. Come on,' he replied.

I felt my stomach flip and didn't resist as he led me out of the hall, across the reception area, through the door, then we leapt down the stone steps to the street.

'This way,' said Niall and we ran round the corner towards Pulteney Bridge then along the pavement towards Parade Gardens. We took the steps down to the garden two at a time again, crossed the grass and Niall stopped by a tree. We stood for a few moments, panting, laughing and catching our breath.

Niall gestured with his hands at the hills to the right of the city, the river roaring behind us, the Abbey to our left. In the clear night sky was a perfect crescent moon.

'You get a good view from down here,' he said.

I nodded. 'I think you do,' I said but instead of looking at the landscape around us, I looked straight at Niall. I could tell by his slow smile that he got my meaning. I turned to look at the scenery. 'I didn't think I'd like Bath when I first moved here.'

Niall's smile became a grin. 'Or anybody in it.'

'Not anybody, just you,' I said cheekily.

'I like to be different and stand out from the crowd.'

'You did.'

'For all the wrong reasons,' said Niall.

'I'm sorry about that. I know about Keiron,' I said. 'I thought you were heckling but I know all about him now.'

'Ancient history,' said Niall. 'But I'm glad that you know I'm not a bully.'

The air around us felt intense and charged with electricity. I knew that we were both thinking the same thing. A first kiss. All of a sudden, I felt nervous. My heart was pounding in my chest and not because we'd been running. I didn't know what to do. Reach up and touch his face? Take his hand? I wished that I could think of something brilliant to say but words seemed to have deserted me. Niall looked into my eyes as if searching for some confirmation of how I was feeling. I didn't look away.

'So. I . . . er, you brought me here to look at the view, huh?' I finally asked.

Niall smiled. 'Not exactly,' he said and continued to look into my eyes. He took control, put his arms around my waist and drew me to him so that I could feel the warmth and weight of his body pressed to me, his eyes not leaving mine for a second. It felt amazing, sensual, right. I closed my eyes and a moment later, I felt his lips, soft, on mine. For a flash, Tasmin's advice about kissing and how to do it came into my mind. But not for long. I didn't need it. Kissing Niall couldn't have felt more perfect. As his kiss grew stronger, it felt as though I was melting into him and feeling the most lovely sensations of warmth and sweetness inside, I'd never experienced anything like it before. As if we were connected body and soul.

When we pulled back from each other, the look that passed between us told me that he'd felt it too. A chance find in a charity shop had led me to him, to this moment, but this was just the beginning and, from the way Niall was still holding me, I knew it was the start of something special.

The House I Loved

TATIANA DE ROSNAY is the author of ten novels, including the *New York Times* bestselling novel *Sarah's Key*, an international sensation with over two million copies sold in thirty-five countries worldwide. Together with Dan Brown, Stephenie Meyer and Stieg Larsson, she was named one of the top ten fiction writers in Europe in 2010. Tatiana lives with her husband and two children in Paris. Visit her online at *www.tatianaderosnay.com*.

Also by Tatiana de Rosnay

Sarah's Key

A Secret Kept